## The road to redemption led through Mission Creek...

Deacon toyed now with the idea of coming clean with the local authorities, telling them who he was and why he was in Mission Creek. But he quickly dismissed the notion as hasty and foolish. No one would believe him anyway. He would have to find that one special person, that one open-minded individual who would be willing to suspend credulity long enough to hear him out. Who would be willing to set aside his or her preconceived notions of reality in order to get at the truth.

Was that someone Marly Jessop?

On first glance, Deacon would have said no. There was a guardedness about her, a self-preservation that suggested she would not easily be coaxed from the safety of her three-dimensional box. And yet something also told him that of all the people in Mission Creek, she might be the only one who could help him find the killer.

Dear Harlequin Intrigue Reader,

We have a superb lineup of outstanding romantic suspense this month starting with another round of QUANTUM MEN from Amanda Stevens. A *Silent Storm* is brewing in Texas and it's about to break....

More great series continue with Harper Allen's MEN OF THE DOUBLE B RANCH trilogy. *A Desperado Lawman* has his hands full with a spitfire who is every bit his match. As well, B.J. Daniels adds the second installment to her CASCADES CONCEALED miniseries with *Day of Reckoning*.

In *Secret Witness* by Jessica Andersen, a woman finds herself caught between a rock—a killer threatening her child—and a hard place—the detective in charge of the case. What will happen when she has to make the most inconceivable choice any woman can make?

Launching this month is a new promotion we are calling COWBOY COPS. Need I say more? Look for *Behind the Shield* by veteran Harlequin Intrigue author Sheryl Lynn. And newcomer, Rosemary Heim, contributes to DEAD BOLT with *Memory Reload*.

Enjoy!

Sincerely,

Denise O'Sullivan
Senior Editor
Harlequin Intrigue

# SILENT STORM
## AMANDA STEVENS

# HARLEQUIN®

TORONTO • NEW YORK • LONDON
AMSTERDAM • PARIS • SYDNEY • HAMBURG
STOCKHOLM • ATHENS • TOKYO • MILAN • MADRID
PRAGUE • WARSAW • BUDAPEST • AUCKLAND

ISBN 0-373-22759-0

SILENT STORM

Copyright © 2004 by Marilyn Medlock Amann

# ABOUT THE AUTHOR

Amanda Stevens is the bestselling author of over thirty novels of romantic suspense. In addition to being a Romance Writers of America RITA® Award finalist, she is also the recipient of awards in Career Achievement in Romantic/Mystery and Career Achievement in Romantic/Suspense from *Romantic Times* magazine. She currently resides in Texas. To find out more about past, present and future projects, please visit her Web site at www.amandastevens.com.

## Books by Amanda Stevens

OKLAHOMA

ARKANSAS

NEW
MEXICO

Dallas
Fort Worth ●

TEXAS          LOUISIANA

Austin
★

Houston
●

San Antonio
●

Mission Creek

N

MEXICO                    Gulf of
                          Mexico

All underlined places are fictitious.

# CAST OF CHARACTERS

**Deputy Marly Jessop**—A killer is on the prowl in Mission Creek, Texas, and the clues lead Marly back to her past.

**Deacon Cage**—His extraordinary skills connect him to the killer.

**Sam Jessop**—What is the secret he's carried with him for years?

**Chief Tony Navarro**—The mysterious lawman has a way with the women.

**Reverend Joshua Rush**—His devotees will do anything to please him.

**Max Perry**—In this time of crisis, the high school counselor has made himself indispensable to the community.

**Colonel Wesley Jessop**—A megalomaniac who always has to be in control.

**Andrea Wesley**—A desperate woman in search of love.

# Chapter One

The rain was relentless. It came down in a steady drizzle, with no let up in sight. Huddled on the front porch of a shabby little house on the outskirts of Mission Creek, Texas, Marly Jessop scanned the gray sky with a growing sense of unease.

Meteorologists were calling it the wettest spring South Texas had seen in over five decades, and they blamed the unusual precipitation on everything from El Niño to global warming. But Marly didn't much care about the science behind the soggy forecast. She had very little knowledge of, or interest in, the upper-level troughs and low pressure systems the so-called experts kept babbling about on the evening news. What she did know was that the dreary weather was starting to wear on her nerves.

The weather…and now the suicides.

Three unnatural deaths in just over a week would be a disturbing phenomenon for any community, but in a town the size of Mission Creek—population 18,733 give or take—it was downright scary.

Wiping a nervous hand down the side of her uniform, Marly turned and knocked on the front door of the wood-frame house. When there was no answer, she gave a quick glance over her shoulder, as if expecting someone to sneak up on her.

But no one was about. The rain had chased everyone inside. The whole community wore an air of abandonment. No passing cars. No barking dogs. No kids playing in puddles.

The only sound came from the raindrops that pattered incessantly against the porch roof, whispered eerily through the citrus trees in the front yard until Marly wanted to lift her hands and cover her ears. The rain was almost like a presence, a ghostly entity that settled over Buena Vista, a blue-collar neighborhood for day laborers, automechanics and construction workers like Ricky Morales, who hadn't been seen or heard from in over three days—according to an anonymous caller—despite the fact that his brand-new Ford pickup was parked underneath the carport.

Marly rapped on the door more insistently. "Ricky? You in there? It's Marly. Marly Jessop. Chief Navarro sent me out here to check up on you. Some of your neighbors are getting worried about you. Come on now. Open up."

Still getting no response, Marly put her ear to the door. She could hear nothing at first over the sound of the rain, but then came the faint tinkle of music. Whether it was coming from inside the house or from somewhere else—her imagination perhaps—Marly didn't know, but the distant strains gave her an eerie sense of déjà vu.

Without warning her mind skidded back in time, and suddenly she was twelve years old again, a gawky adolescent on the cusp of womanhood as she stood on her grandmother's front porch, calling through the door: *"Grandma, you home? It's me, Marlene. I came over to see if you're okay. Mama was worried when you weren't in church this morning. Grandma?"*

There'd been no answer that time, either, just the low, mournful wail of trumpets and the singer's achingly beautiful voice blending with the rain.

The record had been scratched, Marly remembered, so that one part played over and over:

*…Gloomy Sunday…Gloomy Sunday…Gloomy Sunday…*

She could see herself opening the door and stepping inside, her nose wrinkling at the abrasive odor of ammonia that could never quite dispel the old woman scent that permeated the house.

"Grandma?"

Walking quietly down the hallway, Marly glanced over her shoulder to make sure she wasn't leaving muddy footprints on the hardwood floor. Her grandmother hated dirt, almost as much as she despised children. Grubby creatures, she called Marly and her brother, Sam. Unsanitary heathens.

"Grandma?"

*…Gloomy Sunday…Gloomy Sunday…Gloomy Sunday…*

Marly followed the sound of the music up the stairs to her grandmother's bedroom. Hanging from a ceiling beam, the old woman was suspended in a shaft of late-afternoon sunlight. Dust motes danced almost giddily in the air around her, and as Marly stared at the body in horror, she couldn't help thinking how much her grandmother would hate to be found like this. In her own filth, she would call it.

She was missing a shoe, too, and if there was anything Isabel Jessop obsessed over more than her house, it was her appearance. She never wore anything but dresses, all specially made for her by a seamstress in San Antonio. Cotton for everyday and silk or linen for Sundays and special occasions. And she purchased her makeup and toiletries from the cosmetics department at Dillard's. Wonderful smelling concoctions that came in lovely little bottles and jars, which Marly wasn't allowed to touch, let alone sample.

Her grandmother was wearing one of her Sunday dresses now, a crisp lilac linen, and Marly could see the diamond earbobs she'd always coveted glittering from her grandmother's lobes. In the split second before Marly screamed, she wondered what would happen to those earrings now…

…*Gloomy Sunday…Gloomy Sunday…Gloomy Sunday…*

The music faded with the memory, and Marly put a trembling hand to her mouth. Had she really heard that song? Or was her imagination playing tricks on her?

Considering everything that was going on in Mission Creek, it would be understandable if she *had* conjured the melody in her head. Everyone in town was on edge. Miss Gracie's tragic suicide had been hard enough on the community, but then those two high school kids had OD'd four days later.

Marly shuddered. Mission Creek was a small town. She knew all the victims, and their deaths had affected her deeply. And they'd brought back her nightmares with a vengeance.

A wave of dizziness swept over her now, and for a moment, she rested her forehead against the door frame to keep from being sick.

She clenched her fists tightly, willing away the vertigo. This wimpy stuff wasn't going to cut it. She was a peace officer in the township of Mission Creek, in the county of Durango, in the great state of Texas. She was sworn not only to uphold the law, but to serve and protect. If someone inside that house was in trouble, it was her duty to check out the situation and offer assistance. It might not be too late. This time might not be like the other...

But what if it was?

A hand fell on Marly's shoulder, and for a split second, she froze in terror, certain that if she turned, she would find herself staring straight into the sightless eyes of her dead grandmother.

*...Gloomy Sunday...Gloomy Sunday...Gloomy Sunday...*

RAINDROPS POUNDED LIKE A WAR drum on top of Deacon Cage's truck as he headed toward the outskirts of town. Impatiently he reached over the steering wheel to swipe his jacket sleeve across the windshield. He had the defroster going full blast, but the glass kept fogging up on him. And he was cold.

Chilled to the bone even though the outside temperature hovered around sixty.

But the dampness slipped in through the vents, crept underneath the doors and around the windows. It came in like an omen. Like an anxious harbinger sent to warn the good people of Mission Creek that evil had slithered into their town while no one had been watching.

Okay, maybe that was a little on the melodramatic side, Deacon allowed as he glanced at the piece of paper where he'd scribbled an address. Not to mention apocalyptical. But it was hard not to take the weather as a sign given that the rain hadn't let up for weeks.

No wonder there was such a dark, oppressive feel to the town. Deacon had arrived only yesterday and already the weather was getting under his skin.

Spotting his turn just ahead, he slowed, automatically glancing in the rearview mirror before he changed lanes. But there was no one on the wet street behind him. No one around for miles, it seemed. He might have been driving through a ghost town for all the signs of life he saw.

He had the radio turned to a local station, and the newscaster was talking about the suicides. That was all anyone talked about. The suicides and the rain.

Deacon listened for a moment, but there was nothing new in any of the cases. The autopsy reports showed that David Shelley and Amber Tyson, both honor students at Mission Creek High School, had taken lethal doses of a prescription sleeping medication containing benzodiazepine. Their bodies had been found the next morning on a remote road near an abandoned army base.

According to family and close friends, David and Amber were normal teenagers. They weren't loners. They weren't misfits. They didn't have a history of drug use nor were they from broken or abusive homes. By all appearances, they had everything going for them, had bright futures ahead of them. So why had these two "normal" kids suddenly decided to take their own lives?

Why had Gracie Abbott, a seventy-three-year-old retired schoolteacher, who had been planning a trip to Greece in the fall with a favorite niece, driven her car into her garage one gloomy Sunday afternoon, rolled up the windows, and decided to end it all right then and there?

The actions made no sense to those who had known the victims best, but local law enforcement officials maintained that forensic evidence at both crime scenes was consistent with suicide. There was no reason to suspect foul play. After all, some of the highest suicide rates in the country were among the elderly and it was the third leading cause of death in teenagers.

So maybe Deacon was wrong about a connection. About a motive. About everything. He prayed that he *was* wrong.

But he didn't think that he was.

He'd known the moment he crossed the city limits three days ago that something dark and sinister was at work here. A killer was on the prowl, a murderer so cunning that no one in town yet had a clue what they were up against.

But Deacon knew. He knew only too well.

And that was why he was here. The road to redemption led through Mission Creek—and straight to the killer.

"I'm coming for you," he muttered into the silence.

As he made the turn into Buena Vista, a clap of thunder rumbled in the distance, deepening the chill inside his soul.

THE HAND TIGHTENED ON MARLEY'S shoulder, and she whipped around so fast, the person behind her jumped back. The woman lost her footing on the wet porch and would have tumbled down the steps if Marly hadn't grabbed her in the nick of time.

Nona Ferris glared at her accusingly. "What the hell, Marly? You almost knocked me down those steps, girl."

"Sorry. I didn't hear you come up." Marly reached around Nona and rescued the woman's dripping umbrella from the steps, then propped it against the porch wall.

"You sure took your sweet time getting out here," Nona complained. "I called the cops two hours ago."

Marly lifted a brow in surprise. "You're the one who called the station?"

"Yeah, but I never expected them to send you out here alone." Nona carried a pack of cigarettes and lighter in one hand, and now she took a moment to light up. "I thought maybe Navarro would come out here himself."

Was that why she'd called? Marly wondered. It wouldn't be the first time a female citizen of Mission Creek had made a bogus call to the station hoping that Tony Navarro, the chief of police, would put in a personal appearance. He was tall, dark and ruggedly handsome with an enigmatic personality and a mysterious past that had, along with his looks, propelled his reputation to almost mythic proportions in Durango County.

Stifling a sigh, Marly got out her notebook and tried to appear professional. "Well, you know, being the chief of police and all, Navarro has a lot on his plate. I guess he thought I could handle this call myself."

"The least he could do was send one of his deputies," Nona grumbled.

"I am a deputy. See? I have a badge and everything."

Nona cut her a glance. "Not that you don't look real cute in your little Barney Fife uniform, honey, but you know what I mean."

Marly knew what she meant all right. And strangely enough, she wasn't offended by the woman's attitude, probably because she'd known Nona forever. They'd gone to high school together, but in the years since graduation, poor Nona had gotten an advanced degree from the school of hard knocks. She'd once been a pretty girl, but now, dressed in faded yellow sweatpants that sagged in all the wrong places, she was a walking advertisement for too much hooch, sun and cheap hair bleach.

"When you called the station, you told Patty Fuentes that Ricky's been missing for three days," Marly said. "That right?"

"I wouldn't say missing exactly. But something's not right."

"What do you mean?"

Nona gestured with her cigarette. "His truck's been sitting in the carport for three solid days. Now you know Ricky. Even back in high school, he was always a real good worker. Never takes a day off unless he's bad sick."

"Maybe he is sick," Marly suggested. "The flu's going around."

"Too sick to answer his phone? I even went over and hollered through the window at him. Didn't hear a peep out of him."

"Did you try the door?"

"No, but it's not locked," Nona said. "He broke the cheap-ass bolt they put on these houses a long time ago and never did get around to fixing it."

"But you didn't go in and check on him even though you knew the door was unlocked?"

Nona glanced away. "I didn't think that'd be such a hot idea."

"Why not?" Marly asked in surprise. "You and Ricky are still pretty close, aren't you?"

Nona scowled. "What's that supposed to mean?"

"Come on, Nona. You two have been together off and on since high school."

"Yeah, well, now we're just off, okay?" she said

bitterly. "You understand how it is, don't you? Times change. People move on." She gave Marly a knowing look. "Kind of like you and Joshua Rush, I guess."

Marly felt her stomach tighten at the mention of her ex-fiancé. They'd been through for months, but he continued to be a sore subject. She'd never told anyone the details of their breakup, even though people in town were openly curious. They were amazed, Marly suspected, that she'd let a catch like Joshua Rush slip through her fingers. "We were talking about you and Ricky," she reminded Nona.

The woman shrugged. "Not much to tell. We had a falling out not too long ago. A real knock-down drag-out. Ricky warned me not to come around anymore, and considering how he likes to play around with that damn pistol of his, I was afraid the dumb sumbitch might shoot me if I did." She took a long drag on her cigarette. "So that's why I called the cops. Even Ricky'd think twice before plugging the law."

That was some comfort, Marly supposed. She turned back to the door. "I guess I'd better go in and have a look around."

"By yourself?" Nona asked uneasily. "Maybe you ought to call for backup or something."

"It's a little premature for that. Ricky's probably just feeling under the weather—"

"But what if he isn't? What if something bad has happened to him? What if he's—" Nona broke off and glanced away.

Marly narrowed her gaze. "What if he's what?

You don't know something you're not telling me, do you?''

'''Course not.'' Nona gnawed on her thumbnail. ''But after what happened to those kids and old lady Abbott last week, a body can't help being a little nervous.''

''I'm sure it's nothing like that.'' Marly prayed it was nothing like that. She knocked on the door again and called out Ricky's name.

When there was still no answer, she tried the door. It swung open, revealing a dark, cavelike interior. The blinds had been drawn, shutting out what natural light might have come from the overcast sky, and there was a smell. A faint, telltale odor that made Marly's stomach lurch.

She stepped back from the door and tried not to panic.

''Go back over to your house and call Patty,'' she said with far more authority than she actually felt. ''Tell her I may need some help out here. See if she can round up Boyd or A.J. or even the chief. Whoever is nearby.''

A look of dread flashed across Nona's features. ''Ricky…he's not dead in there, is he?''

''Just go make the call, Nona. Hurry up now.''

''But—''

''Go on. This is police business. I know what I'm doing.''

Reluctantly Nona turned, hurried down the steps, then splashed her way across the tiny yard, slipping and sliding on her own wet porch before finally disappearing inside the house a minute or two later.

Marly stepped inside Morales's house, pausing just across the threshold to get her bearings. The front entrance opened directly into the living room, which was separated from the eat-in kitchen on the right by a bar. A windowless door next to the refrigerator led out to the carport, and to the left, a narrow hallway trailed back to the bathroom and bedrooms.

"Ricky? You in here?" she called nervously.

The house was very quiet. Marly couldn't even hear the usual household noises—the humming of the refrigerator, the ticking of a clock. Even the sound of the rain was muffled.

No music, either, she noticed. That was almost a relief.

But…there was something strange about the silence. Something…unnatural. It was as if everything inside Ricky's house had suddenly stopped working.

Resting her hand on her weapon, Marly crossed the room to peer down the murky corridor. "Ricky? It's Deputy Jessop. You in here?"

Still no answer.

Sweat beaded on Marly's forehead as she started down the hallway. The door at the far end was slightly ajar, and as she approached it, the smell grew stronger, making her gag.

Pulling her shirt over her nose and mouth, Marly tried to work up her courage. She had a job to do. She was an officer of the law, and it didn't matter that the most dangerous call she'd been on thus far in her short career with the Mission Creek Police Department was chasing down a pair of ten-year-old shoplifters at the Giant K. All that was about to change, and Marly knew she had to somehow rise to the occasion.

But the smell. She could feel it oozing into her sinuses, into her pores, even into her hair shafts. She'd heard about that smell from some of the veterans who taught at the academy. They'd talked about how it was unmistakable from any other scent, how it was almost impossible to get rid of once it got on you. How you were never able to forget it.

*Don't think about that now,* a little voice warned her.

She tried to put herself on autopilot as she used the toe of her shoe to push open the door. The room was even darker than the rest of the house. She got out her flashlight and switched it on, then played the beam inside the room.

She couldn't say she was surprised by what she found. On some level, she'd been expecting it. Dreading it. Preparing herself for it. But that didn't make the scene any less horrifying.

Ricky Morales lay slumped on the bed, his face mercifully hidden from Marly's view. But the gruesome splatter on the wall just above the headboard told her more than she wanted to know.

# Chapter Two

Staggering back from the room, Marly clapped a hand to her mouth.

*Oh, man. Oh, no.*

She squeezed her eyes closed, trying to ward off the nausea. Trying to block out the revulsion.

But it was too late. She was going to be sick. Collapsing against the wall, she tried to fight it.

*What am I doing here?* she wondered frantically. What had possessed her to enter law enforcement in the first place? She'd never had a burning desire to be a cop. It wasn't some lifelong dream of hers. She wasn't remotely suited for the job, and everyone in town knew it. She'd put in for the opening at the police department because after leaving her last position so abruptly, she'd desperately needed a job. *Any* job.

And then with just eight weeks of training at the Texas Law Enforcement Training Academy in San Antonio under her belt, they'd pinned a badge to her chest, strapped a .38 onto her hips and called her a deputy. But that didn't mean she was qualified. That didn't mean, even after nearly a year on the job, she was equipped to deal with the bloody mess inside that bedroom that had once been Ricky Morales's face—

But she had to deal with it. She had to do something. Call for backup. Secure the scene…

A subtle noise somewhere nearby brought Marly's head up with a jerk. She couldn't tell what the sound was or even where it had come from, but the sudden knowledge that she was no longer alone chilled her blood.

She eased herself away from the wall and for the first time in her short law enforcement career, drew her weapon.

Heart pounding, her mouth dry with fear, she peered down the murky hallway toward the living room.

Someone was there. No doubt about it. She could see his silhouette at the end of the corridor. His features were indistinguishable, but he appeared huge as he started toward her.

Marly clutched her weapon with both hands. "Police! Stay right where you are!"

To her immense relief, the man froze. He didn't so much as move a muscle that Marly could see, but she could feel his gaze on her. Dark. Intense. Cold. Gooseflesh prickled along the back of her neck.

"Hands behind your head," she barked. "No sudden moves."

Slowly he lifted his hands and clasped them behind his head.

Still gripping her weapon, Marly inched toward him. "Who are you?"

"Deacon Cage." His voice was deep and smooth. A little too smooth, Marly decided.

"What are you doing here?" she demanded.

"I'm looking for Ricky Morales."

"He a friend of yours?"

"Not exactly. He didn't show up for work this morning so his boss sent me over here to check up on him."

"This boss have a name?"

"Skip Manson. He's a job foreman for Satterfield Construction. They're building the new gymnasium at the high school."

By this time, Marly was standing only a couple of feet from the stranger, and what she saw when she glanced up caused her heart to skip a beat. Dark hair. Dark eyes. High cheekbones and a well-shaped mouth. A chiseled jawline and a strong, determined chin.

Not bad, Marly thought. Not bad at all.

The stranger lifted a quizzical brow, as if he could tell exactly what she was thinking.

He couldn't, of course, but heat washed over Marly's cheeks just the same. To cover her embarrassment, she gave him a piercing glare. "Do you always enter private residences without an invitation, Mr. Cage?"

"The front door was open. Besides, when I saw the police car out front, I was afraid something might have happened to Morales."

"Like what?"

He shrugged. "An accident maybe."

The way he stared down at her was very unnerving.

*It's like he knows me,* Marly thought with a shiver.

Taking a steadying breath, she tried to disregard the icy tingles shooting through her veins. "I'll need to see some identification."

She tensed when he started to lower his arms.

"I have to get my wallet from my back pocket," he explained.

"Just don't make any sudden moves," she warned.

He fished out his wallet and slowly handed it to her. He was being very cooperative. Nothing in the least threatening about his attitude. So why did she feel so vulnerable? Marly wondered. So…exposed?

She scrutinized the picture on his California driver's license, noting his age, address and physical description. To her dismay, her hand trembled as she folded the wallet and gave it back to him. "You're a long way from home, Mr. Cage."

"No law against that, is there?"

Marly ignored the question. "I'm going to have to ask you to step outside."

"Why? Has something happened to Morales?"

"Just step outside, Mr. Cage."

Something flickered in his eyes, a darkness that made Marly realize how alone they were in the house.

*You have a gun on him. No way he can hurt you.*

But when he made a slight move toward her, Marly jumped back like a nervous cat.

"I wouldn't try that," she warned.

"I'm not going to hurt you."

"Damn straight you're not." She clutched the gun.

He backed off, lifting his hands in acquiescence. "Look, I just want to know what happened here—"

A sound from the living room stopped him cold, and he seemed to grow very tense. "We've got company," he said in that hair-raising voice of his.

Thank God, Marly thought. She wasn't sure how much longer she could take being alone with him. He was a very intimidating man although she had no idea why she felt that way. He hadn't threatened her. Hadn't so much as said anything out of line to her. And yet her instincts told her he was dangerous. In more ways than she could possibly imagine.

Lifting her chin slightly, she tried to peer around him. "Who's there?" she called out. "Identify yourself!"

A slight hesitation, then a male voice responded, "Tony Navarro. Jessop, is that you?"

The stranger jerked around at the sound of Navarro's voice, and he stared down the hall for just a split second before he slowly turned back to face Marly. She caught her breath at the look on his face. If she'd thought him dangerous before, there was no doubt in her mind now. None at all.

What the hell was going on here? she wondered desperately. Who was he? And why was she so afraid of him?

There was something about him, something…not quite of this world. Not with those eyes. That voice…

Marly sucked in a sharp breath as she finally put a name to her fear. He was temptation.

She glanced toward the end of the hallway where Police Chief Tony Navarro had appeared. It might have been Marly's imagination, but she could have sworn the testosterone level in the immediate area shot to a very perilous level.

Even under such grim circumstances, the irony of the situation wasn't lost on her. She hadn't had a date in almost a year, and now all of a sudden she found herself in the company of two tall, dark, dangerously attractive men. The chances of that happening in Mission Creek were slim to none, and just her luck, there was a corpse in the next room.

Chief Navarro was taller than Deacon Cage, but not by much. An inch or two only. His shoulders were a little broader, his hair a little darker, longer, just brushing his collar. He might have had a few years on Cage, too, but in a fair fight, Marly would be hard-pressed to predict a winner. The only sure bet was that both men would battle to the finish.

All this flashed through her mind in the blink of an eye, and in the next instant, when she saw Navarro's hand ease toward his gun, she rushed to say, "It's okay, Chief. Everything's under control here." Quickly she holstered her own weapon.

"What's going on?" He pinned the stranger with a piercing gaze. "Who are you?"

"Deacon Cage." That dark, liquidlike voice sent a fresh tremor through Marly.

She cleared her throat. "Uh, he says he works with Ricky Morales and he came here looking for him—"

"That's not what I said." Deacon's gaze challenged hers. "I said Morales's boss sent me over here to check up on him."

Marly frowned. "I just assumed—"

"First rule of policework," Navarro said slowly, as he started down the hallway toward them. "Never assume anything. You know that as well as I do, Deputy."

Marly's face flamed at her blunder, and she wondered if Deacon Cage had deliberately tried to make her look bad in front of Navarro.

Lifting her chin, she tried to rescue her dignity. "I was just asking Mr. Cage to wait outside, Chief."

Navarro gave the man a curt nod. "Sounds like a good idea. But don't go too far," he advised. "We may have some questions for you."

Deacon Cage hesitated as his gaze traveled from Marly to Navarro and then back to Marly. Lifting a speculative brow, he turned and strode down the hall without a word.

THE FIRST THING DEACON noticed when he stepped outside was that the rain had slackened to a sprinkle. He stood on the porch, listening to the steady *drip-drip* through the trees as he wondered what was going on inside Ricky Morales's house. What kind of scene had Deputy Jessop stumbled upon that had left her looking so pale and shaken?

Deacon had a pretty good idea. After all, he was not unfamiliar with the scent of death. He'd smelled it before, more times than he cared to remember. One might even say he had an intimate relationship with the Grim Reaper.

He toyed with the idea of coming clean with the local authorities, telling them who he was and why he was in Mission Creek. But he quickly dismissed the notion as hasty and foolish. No one would believe him anyway. He would have to find that one special person, that one open-minded individual who would be willing to suspend credulity long enough to hear him out. Who would be willing to set aside his or her preconceived notions of reality in order to get at the truth.

Was that someone Deputy Jessop?

On first glance, Deacon would have said no. There was a guardedness about her, a self-preservation that suggested she would not easily be coaxed from the safety of her three-dimensional box. And yet something also told him that of all the people in Mission Creek, she might be the only one who could help him find the killer.

Or was that merely wishful thinking? Deacon mused. She was an attractive woman in a quiet, unassuming way, and he wouldn't mind spending time with her, although he knew very well it could go nowhere. His stay here was temporary, and as soon as his mission was over, he'd move on. To the next town. To the next killer.

Besides, he came with too much baggage, lived with too many past sins. Slept with too many demons. Demons that would never be exorcised, no matter what he did or how hard he fought for salvation.

But that didn't stop him from trying. That didn't stop him from dreaming about the kind of freedom that was now only a distant memory. A memory he wasn't even sure he could trust.

So here he was. In Mission Creek, Texas. On the trail of yet another killer. Someone who was very much like him. They were all like him in one way or another. And at one time, he'd been like them.

So, no, a relationship with Deputy Marly Jessop—or anyone else—wasn't in the cards for Deacon, and he could allow her to become nothing more to him than a means to an end.

"Hey, you a cop?"

Deacon whirled at the sound of the female voice behind him, annoyed that he hadn't heard her approach. But then he realized it was raining again, and the sound had masked the woman's arrival.

She hurried up the porch steps, her brittle blue gaze openly curious as she gave him a lengthy inspection. She was probably no more than thirty and had once been, Deacon suspected, very pretty in an in-your-face kind of way. But now she had the hardened features of someone who had already experienced a lifetime of disappointment.

"I'm not a cop," Deacon told her.

"Didn't think so. I know all the cops around here, and I've never seen you before." She lit a cigarette and exhaled the smoke on a quick breath. "So who are you, if you don't mind my asking?"

"My name is Deacon Cage."

She propped her right elbow in her left hand, letting the cigarette smolder between her fingers. "I'm Nona. I live across the street." She head-gestured over her shoulder at a little house almost identical to Morales's. "You a friend of Ricky's?"

"Not exactly. But we have a mutual acquaintance."

"A mutual acquaintance, huh?" She gave him a doubtful glance. "Pardon me for saying so, but you don't exactly look like the type Ricky usually hangs out with."

"Well, you know what they say. Appearances can be deceiving."

"Ain't that the damn truth?" Appreciation flashed in her eyes as she gave him another quick assessment. "I saw you come out of the house a few minutes ago. Did you talk to Marly?"

"You mean Deputy Jessop? We spoke briefly."

"What'd she say about Ricky?"

"She wouldn't tell me anything," Deacon replied truthfully.

"Doesn't matter." Nona stared out at the rain, her expression suddenly forlorn. "I already know he's dead."

"How do you know?"

She shrugged, the action not so much one of nonchalance as acceptance. "Because people are dropping like flies around here."

"You mean the suicides?" Deacon asked carefully.

"You know what I think?" She gave him an anxious look. "I think it's the weather. All this damn rain. It's depressing as hell. Enough to make anyone wacko." She grimaced. "Marly must be freaking out, though."

"Because of the weather?"

Nona glanced back at the rain. "No, because of the suicides."

"What do you mean?"

She hesitated. "Let's just say, Marly has some issues and leave it at that, okay?"

What kind of issues? Deacon wanted to ask, but he didn't press her. He had a feeling Nona was a woman who liked to talk, and with a little patience, he'd find out everything he wanted to know from her without having to resort to anything...drastic. "You sound as if you know Deputy Jessop pretty well."

Nona shrugged again. "Not really. We went to high school together, but we didn't exactly hang out with the same crowd, if you know what I mean. Marly was the straight-A-honor-roll type of girl while I was—" She broke off and gave him a sidelong glance. "You might say I had a different set of priorities in high school."

Deacon nodded. "Fair enough."

"I sure as hell never would have pictured her as a cop, though."

"Why not?"

Nona watched a cloud of smoke drift off the

porch. "She's just not cut out for it. Too much of a goody-goody. Let's people push her around all the time. Especially her old man."

"Her husband?"

Nona shook her head. "She's not married. No, I'm talking about her father. He's a retired army colonel. Used to be the base commander over at Fort Stanton before it closed. Not exactly Mr. Personality, if you get my drift. I knew some of the guys who were stationed there, and they hated his guts. Said he was one mean son of a bitch." She paused to take another drag on her cigarette, then expelled the smoke on a nervous laugh. "I don't mean to bend your ear like this. It's just...I have a tendency to talk too much when I get jittery." She tossed the cigarette butt over the porch railing and watched it sizzle in the wet grass. "Smoke too much, too."

"I don't mind. I'm enjoying our conversation," Deacon said.

"Yeah?" Her gaze turned speculative as she gave him another careful once-over.

"You were telling me about Marly Jessop's father, the retired army colonel," he gently coaxed.

Nona nodded. "My mother used to be their housekeeper, see. That's how come I know so much about them. She's got stories about that family that could curl your hair, let me tell you. She always felt real bad for Marly and Sam, though."

"Sam?"

"Marly's brother."

"Does he live here in Mission Creek?"

"He came back here after he left the service. He's

moved into their grandmother's old place. Really got it fixed up nice. I even noticed when I drove by there the other day that he has the garage apartment up for rent. Not that I'm interested, mind you." She gave an exaggerated shudder. "You couldn't pay me enough. Even if it would mean getting to see Sam every day, and that's saying something for me. Always did have a thing for him."

Deacon worked to keep his expression neutral. "You say he was in the service? Which branch?"

"The army, just like his father and grandfather. The grandfather was some big shot general at the Pentagon or something. Sam was supposed to follow in their footsteps, but he quit after a few years and came back here to teach school. From what I hear, the old man nearly had a stroke over it. But Mama said he always did try to run those kids' lives. Stayed on their cases all the damn time. They never could do anything right. I guess it's no wonder Marly turned out the way she has."

"What do you mean?"

Nona thought for a moment. "She's just… different. She has this way about her. Kind of like…she knows things the rest of us don't? It's hard to explain, but I guess being strange runs in that family when you consider what her grandmother did." She leaned toward Deacon and lowered her voice. "Remember what I said about Marly having issues?"

He nodded.

"Well, old lady Jessop hanged herself when

Marly was just twelve. Marly was the one who found the body. I don't think she ever got over it.''

"Be hard to get over something like that," Deacon muttered.

Nona lit up another cigarette. "Kind of creepy when you think about it, though. Marly was the one who found her grandmother all those years ago, and now here she is a cop, having to investigate all these other suicides. That's what I call a really weird-ass coincidence.''

Weird maybe. But Deacon didn't really believe in coincidences.

# Chapter Three

Dr. Alvin Pliner, the Durango County medical examiner, snapped on a pair of latex gloves as he approached the corpse with what Marly perceived as an unseemly amount of enthusiasm. Here was a man who clearly enjoyed his job, she thought with a shudder.

"You've protected the crime scene, I assume." He made the prospect sound doubtful.

"Don't worry, it's virgin," Navarro assured him. He gave Marly a slight wink at the medical examiner's pomposity, and her stomach fluttered uncomfortably. Navarro had that kind of effect. He was the epitome of tall, dark, and handsome, and the .357 Magnum he wore strapped to his hip gave him a certain bad-ass cachet that was downright irresistible.

All the women in town were half in love with him, but no one really knew much about him. An ex-Navy SEAL, he'd come to Mission Creek a little over a year ago to meet with the mayor and the city council, and whatever had gone down in those closed-door sessions had convinced them to hire him on the spot as the new chief of police.

From the very first, he'd been a different kind of cop than his predecessor. Boyd Hendrickson had been an aging lawman who had been all too content to coast along until his retirement. No one could accuse Navarro of complacency. He took an active role in every investigation, but he also remained somewhat of an outsider in the department, eschewing the standard uniform for jeans, boots, and on chilly days like today, a black leather jacket that made him seem cool, aloof and more than a little dangerous.

Marly dropped her gaze and tried to focus on Dr. Pliner as he moved his gloved hands with quick efficiency over the body. "He's dead all right. Did you notice the blowback on his right hand? GPR is going to turn up positive, I can almost guarantee."

"So you think it's another suicide," Navarro said quietly.

"Lucky Number Four," Pliner agreed. "Although not so lucky for this poor bastard. I'll be able to tell you more about time of death after the autopsy."

He continued to poke and prod the corpse until Marly, still in danger of losing the contents of her stomach, had to leave the room. She walked down the hall into the living area and stood gazing around.

The room was sparsely furnished with a battered old sofa and recliner arranged around a small TV. The walls were decorated with Houston Astros and Harley-Davidson memorabilia, and the dining room table was strewn with mechanical parts, probably from the vintage Harley she'd seen under the carport. Marly could picture Ricky sitting there at night, listening to a baseball game on TV while he painstakingly restored and rebuilt piece by piece what had undoubtedly been his pride and joy.

Being in his house, examining his personal belongings was a little too much like having a glimpse into the man's private dreams, Marly thought. She didn't want to poke and prod into every aspect of his life, rip away the last vestiges of his dignity. All she really wanted was to go home, climb into a hot shower and wash that awful scent from her hair and from her skin. And from her memory, if possible.

She wasn't like Navarro. She wasn't the kind of cop who could walk away from a gruesome scene and put it out of her mind. Ricky Morales's death would eat at her. His sightless eyes would haunt her sleep for years to come.

Handing out traffic citations was one thing, but all these deaths...

Marly hadn't signed on for anything like this, and she toyed with the idea of handing in her resignation. She could just walk out the door and not look back, and no one would really be all that surprised. If anything, the people who knew her best were shocked that she'd stuck it out for this long.

*Quitter,* a voice inside her taunted. A voice that sounded very much like her father's.

Well, better a quitter who could sleep at night, Marly reasoned.

Navarro had once told her that she had what it

took to be a good cop. She had all the right instincts, he'd said. But did she have the guts?

It was a good question, and one Marly still wasn't sure she could answer. Especially now, when her instincts were telling her something she didn't want to hear.

Something bad was happening in Mission Creek. Something…evil.

And Marly didn't have a clue how to fight it.

WHEN DEPUTY JESSOP FINALLY emerged from the house, she hurried down the porch steps without even a glance in Deacon's direction. For a moment, it looked as if she were fleeing from the devil himself, and Deacon wondered if he should follow her. Find out what the hell was going on. But then one of the police officers who'd arrived on the scene just after the medical examiner called out to her and she paused. She turned and—reluctantly it seemed to Deacon—walked over to consult with her colleague.

Deacon studied her carefully, noting the flicker of emotions across her face, the almost convulsive movement of her hands. He remembered what Nona had said about her earlier, that she wasn't cut out to be a cop. She was too much of a goody-goody. She let people push her around.

Maybe.

But in the few moments they'd stood talking in the hallway, Deacon had glimpsed something that made him think there was more to Marly Jessop than met the eye. She possessed the kind of innate courage that had allowed her to stand her ground even in the face of what she had obviously perceived as grave danger. That courage was buried deep, he suspected, but it was there, nonetheless. And if he was right about the nature of these recent deaths, she would need every ounce she could muster in the coming days. They both would.

As if sensing his scrutiny, Marly glanced up and their gazes met across the yard before she quickly looked away. But in that moment, something passed between them. Attraction—at least on Deacon's part—but something else, too. A flash of understanding or perhaps even precognition that their paths had crossed for a reason.

Lifting a hand to the back of her neck, Marly continued to speak with the other officer. After a moment, he returned to his squad car and drove off while she sloshed back over to the porch.

Nona, who had been smoking quietly as she observed the exchange in the yard, tossed her cigarette over the rail. "You gonna finally tell us what happened to Ricky or what?"

Marly climbed the steps slowly. "I'm sorry, Nona. Ricky's dead."

"I already know that." Nona's tone was hard as nails, but her eyes glittered with emotion. "I want to know how it happened."

Marly's gaze slid to Deacon's. "Nona, would you mind waiting for me at your house? I need to have a word with Mr. Cage here." When the woman started to protest, Marly laid a hand on her sleeve. "I'll come over as soon as I'm finished and tell you what I can."

Nona sighed. "All right, but don't leave me hanging, okay? Ricky and I go way back. We may've had our differences, but I've got a right to know what happened to him."

Marly waited until Nona had exited the porch before she turned back to Deacon. She tilted her head to gaze up at him, and Deacon realized suddenly how tiny she was. How young she looked with her dark blond hair chopped off short and plastered to her head. She wore no makeup, and the freckles that dotted the bridge of her nose gave her a wholesome, girl-next-door look. But her eyes—an odd shade of gold—reflected a hint of bitterness that made Deacon wonder about her past.

Something tightened inside him, and not for the first time, he wished he was someone—or something—other than who he was. He wished he was the type of man who could have a woman like Marly Jessop.

He *could* have her. He had the power to make her his. All he had to do was look deeply into those golden eyes and make her want him. Make her believe that she couldn't live without him, that she would do anything in the world to have him. And just like that, she would be his.

For a little while. Until she learned the truth about him.

Then she would hate him. And she would have every right.

Reluctantly he broke eye contact and turned his gaze to the rain. Beside him, Marly stirred restlessly, as if sensing more than he wanted her to.

"Why'd you come back?" he asked softly.

She glanced at him in surprise. "I beg your pardon?"

He nodded toward the street. "You were leaving, weren't you? Running away? What made you come back?"

Anger flashed in her eyes. "You don't know me, Mr. Cage, so don't presume you understand anything about me. Besides, I'm here to ask the questions."

He gave a brief nod. "Go ahead then."

"What are you doing in Mission Creek? What's your business here?"

"I'm just passing through."

"On your way to…?"

He shrugged. "West."

One brow lifted. "West of Mission Creek? West of Texas? West encompasses a lot of territory."

"I'm not exactly sure what my plans are. But I do know that I'm not breaking any laws by being here."

Her features tightened. "You're always quick to point that out, aren't you? If I were the suspicious type, I might think you have a guilty conscience."

"Am I under suspicion for something?" he asked bluntly.

Her gaze faltered, but she still didn't look away. "No. I am a little curious about the way you turned up here, though."

"I explained all that. Morales's boss sent me over here to check up on him."

"Why you?"

He shrugged. "I stopped by the construction site to inquire about work. I'd heard around town they were hiring."

Marly frowned. "You're looking for work here? Sounds like you intend to stay awhile."

"As I said, I don't have any firm plans at the moment. But I can always use the extra cash." Her eyes were very expressive, Deacon thought. And very beautiful. Like pools of liquid gold.

Her scowl deepened. "So you stopped by the job site to ask about work, and the foreman sent you over here to check up on Ricky. Just out of the blue?"

"He mentioned that Morales hadn't been showing up for work. He was worried about him, but he couldn't take the time to come over here himself."

"So you volunteered."

Deacon stared down at her. "Never hurts to get in good with the boss, right?"

Something flickered in her eyes, a tiny embarrassment that made Deacon remember how she'd looked when Navarro had first arrived on the scene. Nervous. Disconcerted. Her voice had been breathless when she'd called out to him. Was there something going on between them?

Not that it would matter in the long run. But it might make what Deacon had to do a little more difficult if she was involved with someone.

Marly's gaze turned suddenly defiant, as if she'd somehow sensed what he was up to. "I don't know who you are or why you're here," she muttered.

"But something tells me I'm not getting the whole truth out of you yet."

"Does it matter why I'm here?" He looked into her eyes. Tried to peer all the way into her soul. "You have more important things to worry about, don't you? There've been four suicides in your town in a ten-day period. I'd say you've got bigger problems than me, Deputy."

"You think I don't know that?" she snapped. "But I never said Ricky Morales committed suicide."

"You didn't have to." Deacon watched her for a moment. "I can help you, Marly."

"What are you talking about? Help me how?" Her tone was indignant.

"You and I both know these suicides aren't what they seem."

A shadow flickered in her eyes, and for a moment, she looked as if she was on the verge of agreeing with him. Then her rational side took over and her resolve hardened. "There's no reason to suspect foul play. Forensic evidence at every one of the scenes—"

"Is consistent with suicide. Yes, I know. I'm not suggesting these people didn't die by their own hand. I have no doubt that Gracie Abbott drove her car into her garage, rolled up all the windows and let the carbon monoxide do its job. I'm certain those two kids purposely took overdoses and Ricky Morales pulled that trigger. What I am suggesting is that they were somehow compelled to do it."

Marly gave him an incredulous look. "*Com-*

*pelled?* How on earth do you compel someone to commit suicide?''

"It's been done before," Deacon said. "A man named Jim Jones led more than nine hundred of his followers to their deaths at Jonestown, Guyana, by drinking a cyanide-laced punch. Thirty-nine Heaven's Gate devotees were found dead in a mansion near San Diego, California. I could go on, but I think you get my point.''

A myriad of emotions flashed across Marly's features. Revulsion. Horror. Disbelief. But she didn't turn away. She didn't send him packing. She was listening whether she wanted to or not. "You're not suggesting something like that is going on here, are you?''

"I'm suggesting you need to keep an open mind if you want to stop this.''

She tore her gaze from his and stared across the yard where a small crowd had gathered on the sidewalk. A breeze whispered through the orange trees in the front yard, and overhead, the rain beat a steady staccato on the porch roof.

It was a long time before she spoke. And even then, she avoided his gaze, as if sensing eye contact with him could be a dangerous thing. She watched the rain with a brooding frown. "In those cases you cited, the bodies were all found together. It's happening one at a time here. And the incidents appear unrelated. An elderly woman. Two teenagers. A construction worker. Where's the connection?''

"That's what we have to find out," Deacon said. ''*We?*''

"Like I said, I can help you."

He saw her shiver at the prospect. "If you have information regarding any of these deaths, you should take it to Chief Navarro. He's heading up the investigations."

"I'm telling you, Marly. Because you know something bad is happening is this town. You know something's not right about these deaths. I can see it in your eyes." His gaze challenged hers. "And whether you want to admit it or not, you may be the only one who can stop it."

DEACON FIDDLED WITH THE RADIO dial in his truck as he kept an eye on the front porch of Ricky Morales's house. After his conversation with Marly, he'd left the scene at her rather adamant insistence, circled the block a couple of times, then pulled his truck to the curb a few houses down where he could unobtrusively observe the comings and goings of the authorities.

A hearse from a local funeral home had arrived on the scene just after Deacon had left which meant they would soon bring out the body. Onlookers mingled on the sidewalk, and Deacon knew that word would soon be all over town about Morales's death. In a day or two, the autopsy would confirm suicide, and the case would be closed. There would be lingering speculation, of course, but no one in Mission Creek would seriously suspect homicide. No one except Deacon…and now Marly Jessop.

She was still standing on the front porch, speaking to another deputy. Deacon couldn't see her features through the rain, but he remembered all too vividly the nuances of her face—those golden eyes, those lips that were neither thin nor full but lush, none-theless, and pliant, he somehow knew. He imagined running his thumb along that mouth, then tasting her with his tongue, teasing and coaxing until she opened like a flower beneath him.

Did she have any idea how attractive she was? How sensual? Deacon knew instinctively that she was a complicated woman, and he wondered if any man had ever taken the time to really know her. If any man had taken the time to nurture her latent passion into full bloom.

Because she was a passionate woman, he thought. Beneath her cool, almost nondescript façade he'd glimpsed an ember, a tiny, ardent flame just waiting to be stoked, by a patient hand, into a raging inferno of needs and desires.

He rubbed a hand across his eyes, trying to erase the vision of an aroused Marly Jessop. That kind of thinking was dangerous because it could make him lose sight of the mission. He was here for one reason only. To stop a killer, and to do so, he needed Marly's help. Beyond that, his feelings for her couldn't be allowed to matter.

But what if she refused to help him? What if he couldn't make her accept the truth?

He had ways of gaining her cooperation, of course. Ways of convincing her. But afterward, she would never trust him again.

Well, so be it, he decided grimly.

The cell phone on the truck seat rang and he lifted it to his ear. "Cage."

"Deacon, it's Camille."

At the sound of his colleague's voice, Deacon tensed. "What's wrong?"

"Grandfather—"

"He's worse?" Deacon's hand tightened on the phone.

"No, no, it's not that," Camille rushed to assure him. "He just wanted to make sure you're okay. He has a bad feeling about this job, Deacon."

Deacon let out a breath of relief. "He has a bad feeling about every job."

"I know. It's because…he feels we're running out of time."

Deacon sometimes felt that way, too. There were so many of them out there. A secret army of soldiers who had been trained and programmed to kill…and couldn't stop.

And Deacon had once been one of them.

He didn't like to contemplate what his life might have been like if Dr. Nicholas Kessler, a renowned quantum physicist, and his granddaughter hadn't found him when they had. Hadn't recruited him to the good side as Camille liked to tease him.

"As much as it pains me to admit it, Grandfather isn't going to be around forever," she said. "He'll be eighty-nine his next birthday."

"And still as sharp as ever," Deacon reminded her.

"His mind, yes, but his body is failing him, Deacon. You know how frail he is. I can't help worrying what will happen to our work when he's gone.''

Deacon shrugged. ''We'll carry on as we have been.''

''You'll take over the organization when the time comes?'' she asked anxiously.

''You're more qualified to run it than I am,'' he said with a frown. ''Besides, I like being in the field.''

''I know you do. And that's what worries me because one of these days…''

''One of these days, what?''

She hesitated. ''One of these days you may meet your match out there.''

''That's not going to happen.'' But Deacon knew it could easily happen because on every mission the killer always had the advantage. He was on his home turf, and the only way for Deacon to even the odds was to recruit someone locally to help him. Someone like Marly Jessop.

He said none of that to Camille, however, because she tended to be a worrier and she had too much on her plate as it was. She was right. Her grandfather might not last much longer, and when the time came, Nicholas's death would hit her hard. She'd lost her only child not so long ago, and though she put up a brave front, Deacon knew she hadn't recovered from the blow. Her grandfather and her work were all she had left.

And at that, she had a damn sight more than Deacon.

''So how are things going down there?'' she

asked, and Deacon could tell she was deliberately changing the subject.

"There's been another death," he said, his gaze riveted to the front of Ricky Morales's house. They were bringing out the body. He watched as they hauled the stretcher down the steps and across the soggy yard to the hearse. Marly was talking to Navarro now, and Deacon frowned. There was something about her body language...something about the way she looked up at her superior...

"Deacon?"

He gritted his teeth and glanced away. "Yeah, I'm still here. I'm at the scene now."

"Is it...a suicide?"

"There's suicide and there's suicide," he said.

"Yes, I know." Deacon could picture her seated behind her computer, dark hair pulled back and fastened primly at her nape as she scowled at her screen. Her full lips would be pursed in concentration, her violet eyes shadowed with a grief that had only deepened in the months since her son's death. "Do you have any leads?"

"Nothing concrete. I have a couple of names I'd like you to run through the usual databases, though. I don't expect anything to turn up, but you never know. The first one is Tony Navarro. He's the chief of police down here."

"Any particular reason you're interested in him?"

Deacon's gaze went back to the couple on the porch. "Just a gut instinct."

"You really think the chief of police could be one

of them?'' Camille persisted. She must have sensed something in his voice. Sometimes her instincts were uncanny.

"One of *us,* you mean?'' Deacon countered.

She hesitated. "You know I don't think of you that way. Besides, not everyone who went through Montauk was or is a killer. Some of the men have even gone back to their normal lives.''

"Yeah,'' Deacon said. "And some of them are in psychiatric wards. Some of them are living on the streets.'' And some of them had continued to kill.

"You said there were two names,'' Camille prompted.

"The other is Sam Jessop. I haven't met him yet, but from everything I've learned, he matches the profile. He was in the army, and he comes from a military family.''

"Okay. I'll check them out and get back to you. Anything else?''

"There's an abandoned army base not far from here. See what you can dig up about it.''

He heard her catch her breath. "You don't think it was part of Montauk, do you?''

"We know they expanded the operation,'' Deacon said. "And we've never discovered the other locations. It's worth checking out.''

"That should keep me busy for a day or two,'' Camille said. "In the meantime, keep in touch, okay? Grandfather worries about you. So do I,'' she added reluctantly.

Deacon's features tightened. "I wish you wouldn't. I don't deserve it.''

Camille sighed. "You're never going to get past it, are you?"

A muscle began to pulse in Deacon's jaw. "Get past who I am? What I did?"

"You were following orders," Camille said. "You were programmed to—"

"Kill people."

"You don't know that for sure."

"Face it, Camille. Just because I can't remember doesn't mean it didn't happen. I was an assassin. You don't move on from something like that. There's no redemption for what I did."

"There might be," she said softly. "If you could somehow find it in your heart to forgive yourself."

## Chapter Four

Nona had left her front door open, and as Marly climbed the porch steps a few minutes later, she could hear the woman banging around inside.

She walked up to the door and called through the screen. "Nona?"

"It's open!"

Marly glanced around as she stepped inside. The layout of the house was almost identical to the one across the street. The front door opened directly into a small, cramped living area decorated in country blue. Perky gingham curtains with crisp sashes hung from the windows while an army of bonneted geese marched in single file across a ceiling border.

The homey décor surprised Marly although she'd really had no idea what to expect. Nona's mother had once worked for her family, but Marly was ashamed to admit that she'd never really taken the time to know Nona or Mrs. Ferris.

But it wasn't because she was a snob. Far from it. Truth be told, Marly had always been a little in- timidated by Nona's brassy good-looks and her rather disconcerting habit of speaking her mind without regard to the consequences.

She'd been one of the bad girls in high school, running with a crowd that had voraciously smoked, drank, or popped whatever drug they could get their hands on at the moment. They'd gone to raves every weekend, skipped school every Monday, and generally didn't give a damn what anyone in town thought of them. Marly had envied their freedom.

Even now, with the evidence of all that hard living etched poignantly in Nona's face, Marly suspected the woman still managed to live life on her own terms. She might not be particularly happy with the hand she'd been dealt, but she accepted it and made no excuses or apologies for it.

And Marly still envied her.

"Well?" Nona demanded from the kitchen. "Are you going to stand there all damn day or are you going to tell me about Ricky?"

Marly walked over to the bar and pulled out a stool. "Sorry. I was just admiring your house."

Nona gave a derisive snort. "Yeah, right."

"No, seriously." Marly glanced around. "It's really warm and cozy. I like it."

Nona shrugged. "Well, thanks. But it's hardly in the same league as your house."

"I don't have a house," Marly said. "I live in an apartment."

"I meant your parents' place."

Cozy and warm were not adjectives Marly would ever use to describe the house where she'd grown up. The split-level ranch, decorated so meticulously and beautifully by her mother, had always seemed cold and unwelcoming. Oppressive.

"You want some coffee?" Nona grabbed two cups from the dish drainer by the sink and placed them on the counter.

Marly shook her head. "No, thanks."

"You sure? It's fresh. I just made it," Nona said as she poured herself a cup.

"I'm not much of a coffee drinker," Marly told her.

"A Coke then? Some juice?"

"I'm fine." Marly's gaze fastened on a flyer that had been tossed on the counter. Even before she scanned the text advertising an old-fashioned revival meeting at a local church, she knew the leaflet had come from the Glorious Way on Sixth Street. Joshua Rush's church. The emblem on the front was unmistakable. The rays of light emanating from an eye symbolized enlightenment—or so Joshua had once told her.

For some reason, that eye made Marly a little uneasy, probably because she now knew Joshua's true, pathological nature.

Noticing her gaze, Nona said, "Someone slipped that under my door the other day. I guess they're trying to tell me something."

Marly smiled. "I wouldn't take it personally. They're probably passing out those leaflets all over the neighborhood."

"Maybe." Nona picked up her cup, cradling the thick ceramic mug in both hands as if she were suddenly chilled. "So tell me about Ricky. What happened to him?"

"The medical examiner will make the final determination as to cause of death," Marly said. "So what I'm about to tell you isn't for public consumption. Keep it to yourself until there's an official announcement, okay?"

Nona nodded, but her expression seemed doubtful. She would probably talk, Marly thought, but it didn't really matter. Everyone in town would know about Ricky's death in a matter of hours. Already a crowd had gathered on the street outside his house.

"It looks like Ricky died from a gunshot wound," she said.

"Son of a bitch." Nona let out a shaky breath. "I used to worry about him hurting someone with that damn pistol of his, but I never thought he'd up and shoot himself."

"I never said it was suicide," Marly said quickly.

"It was, though, wasn't it?" Nona wrapped her arms around her middle. "What the hell is going on in this damn town anyway? Why are all these people killing themselves? Why Ricky?"

Marly lifted her shoulders helplessly, but she couldn't help wondering the same thing. Could Deacon Cage be right? Was there someone in town, someone she knew, who could *compel* people to commit suicide?

Her gaze lit on the flyer again, and an uneasy shiver crept up her backbone. "I'm no expert on human behavior," she tried to say evenly. "It's going to take us a while to figure it all out, I guess. In the meantime, I need to ask you some questions about Ricky. Is that all right with you?''

"What kind of questions?'' Nona asked with a frown.

"Just routine.'' Marly got out her notebook. "You said the two of you had a recent falling out. Tell me about that.''

"If you're thinking that might be the reason Ricky killed himself, no way. He wasn't losing any sleep over our breakup,'' Nona said bitterly.

"How do you know?''

"Because he had himself a new girlfriend. I walked in on them one night. He was…entertaining her on the living room couch. Couldn't even make it to the bedroom.'' Her voice was edged with lingering anger and hurt. "We had words. Things got a little out of hand. I ended up tossing her clothes out the front door, and then Ricky threw me out. Told me it was over between us, he was in love with someone else, and I'd better leave them alone if I knew what was good for me.'' She sniffed and drew a hand across her nose.

"When was the last time you saw him?''

Nona thought for a moment. "Last Saturday night. I met some friends for drinks at that new country and western place out on Highway Seven. Used to be the Tin Roof. Anyway, Ricky was there with Crystal.''

Marly glanced up sharply. "Crystal.''

"Crystal Bishop, the new girlfriend. She's Gus Bishop's niece. You know, the high school custodian? I'd bet good money that creepy old bastard has dirt on somebody over there because I don't know how else Crystal could have ended up working in the school office. Her experience is not exactly clerical in nature, if you know what I mean.''

Yes, Marly thought with her own unexpected bitterness. She knew only too well where Crystal Bishop's talents lay.

She remembered, with vivid clarity, the day she'd found the woman in Joshua's office, the way Crystal's long, black hair had cascaded down her tanned back...how her slim, nude body had moved rhythmically as her cries mingled with Joshua's...

Marly had stood frozen in place, too shocked to move let alone speak. Crystal's back had been to her, but Joshua, sprawled beneath her on the sofa, had spotted Marly in the doorway. He hadn't looked particularly surprised to find her there and certainly not repentant. He'd merely encircled Crystal's waist and lifted her off him, but not before—Marly would have sworn—he'd finished.

She was annoyed now to find that the memory still rankled—not because she harbored feelings for Joshua Rush—but because, for a short time, she'd allowed him to have power over her.

But that was all in the past, she reminded herself. And it had been a lesson well learned.

"What else you want to know about Ricky?" Nona prompted.

Marly forced her attention back to the conversation. "Did you talk to him on Saturday night?"

Nona shook her head. "No. I didn't stay long. Luanne MacAllister dropped me off here before ten.

Ricky came in around midnight. I heard his truck pull into the carport.''

"How can you be sure about the time?" Marly asked her.

"*Saturday Night Live* was just going off. I don't usually watch the whole show, but I did that night because Matthew McConaughey was the host, and I've got a real thing for him. He kind of reminds me of your brother.''

"Do you know if Ricky was alone?''

"I'm pretty sure he was. I happened to look out the window, and I didn't see anyone with him.''

"You didn't see or hear anything out of the ordinary that night?''

Nona gave her a knowing look. "You mean like a gunshot? No, but that doesn't mean anything. Takes me a while to fall asleep, but when I do, it's like waking the dead.''

"Was that the last time you saw Ricky?''

She nodded. "His truck was in the carport all the next day, but it was Sunday so I didn't think anything of it. I just figured he was hungover or something and didn't feel like getting out. When I saw his truck was still there on Monday, I thought maybe his crew had gotten rained out. But then I ran into one of his buddies at the Giant K this morning, and he said the crew was far enough along on the new gym that the weather wasn't a problem. They were mostly working inside now. Anyway, that got me to thinking that maybe I'd better get the cops out here to check up on him.''

"Were you home all weekend?''

Nona nodded. "I'm without wheels at the moment, so yeah, I was home."

"You didn't see anyone come in or out of Ricky's house?"

"No."

"No strange cars in the neighborhood?"

Nona looked startled. "What are you getting at, Marly?"

"I'm just covering all the bases."

Nona's eyes were like saucers. "You don't think someone *murdered* Ricky, do you?"

"Like I said, these are just routine questions. Nothing to be alarmed about." But Marly wasn't certain if she was trying to convince Nona or herself. "How did Ricky seem to you on Saturday night?"

"Okay, I guess. But I got the impression he and Crystal weren't exactly getting along. If you think someone killed poor Ricky, maybe you better go talk to her."

Marly intended to, but it wasn't a conversation she looked forward to. She closed her notebook and stood. "That should do it for now. Thanks for your cooperation, Nona."

She shrugged. "Least I could do for Ricky. Like I said, we had our differences, but we go way back." She came around the counter and walked Marly to the door.

"I'll be in touch. As soon as we hear back from the medical examiner, I'll let you know." Marly opened the screen door, but before she could step outside, Nona put a hand on her arm.

"Marly?"

She turned.

Nona bit her lip, looking for the world like a woman who needed to get something off her chest.

"What is it, Nona?" Marly urged gently.

"You want to hear something…weird?"

"What?"

Nona hugged her arms to her chest. "I've been having these really crazy-ass dreams lately. I didn't think much about them at first, but now after what happened to Ricky—" She broke off, her gaze moving past Marly to the open front door. Her uneasiness was so palpable Marly suddenly had the urge to glance over her shoulder.

"What kind of dreams?" she asked.

Nona glanced away. "I've been dreaming about…hurting myself."

Marly tried to hide her shock. "What?"

The words tumbled out of Nona. "I have this real sharp knife in my hand, see, the kind Daddy used to take hunting. You know, to skin rabbits and stuff. Anyway, I'm moving it toward my wrist. Real slow like." She demonstrated with her finger.

Marly stared at the woman's wrist in fascination, watching Nona's finger move closer and closer to the vein.

"I know what's about to happen, but I can't stop. It's like…something's making me do it," Nona whispered.

*What I am suggesting is that they were somehow compelled to do it.*

A chill raced up Marly's spine. "Everyone dreams crazy stuff." She'd certainly had her fair share of nightmares lately. "It's only natural with everything that's going on around here."

"I know, but..." Nona's blue gaze met Marly's. "What freaks me out is...I had that dream on Saturday night, probably just about the time Ricky was pulling that trigger."

CRYSTAL BISHOP STARED at her reflection in the mirror and smiled. She had every reason to be pleased with herself, she decided. She was finally back where she belonged—in Joshua Rush's life and in his bed. And if she had her say in the matter, she wouldn't be leaving anytime soon.

Of course, if she'd had her way, she never would have left in the first place. Their separation had been all Joshua's doing. After the tacky scene with Marly in his office that day, he'd been worried about what she might tell people, the rumors she might spread about him out of spite. And in his line of work, Joshua couldn't afford even a breath of scandal.

So he'd convinced Crystal that the two of them had to play it cool and keep their distance until the breakup with Marly blew over. He had to have—what had he called it?—plausible deniability if she started flinging around accusations.

But to Crystal's surprise, Marly hadn't said a word to anyone about what she'd seen that day. Crystal wasn't so sure if she'd been in Marly's shoes that she would have been so discreet. But then, finding her fiancé in bed with a younger, prettier, sexier woman probably wasn't something Marly wanted to get around.

Crystal fluffed her dark hair, her smile slipping a bit as she remembered how weeks had gone by and then months before Joshua had finally gotten around to calling her. If she hadn't hooked up with Ricky, she wasn't so sure Joshua would have ever come around, but he couldn't stand the thought of another man sampling what he considered his.

At the thought of Ricky Morales, Crystal's smile disappeared altogether and she sighed. He'd become a problem toward the end. A real pain. What was supposed to be a casual fling—and had remained so for her—had turned into something serious for Ricky. He'd fallen in love with her, had even asked her to marry him, and when he'd caught her with Joshua—

Crystal shuddered, remembering the awful scene. Unlike Marly, Ricky wasn't about to keep his mouth shut. He'd even threatened Joshua and that had terrified Crystal, not so much because she was worried about what Ricky might do, but because the gossip might drive Joshua away again.

But Joshua had merely told her to take care of the problem. And she had. Last Saturday night. She hadn't wanted to do it. She took no pleasure in hurting Ricky. It was kind of like torturing a kitten. He was a real sweet guy, but she wouldn't risk her future for him. No way was she going to end up back in Buena Vista. She wanted someone more sophisticated. More worldly. Someone who was going places. Someone like Joshua Rush.

Besides, Ricky—for all his willingness to please her—had been, to put it mildly, sexually incurious.

She certainly couldn't say that about Joshua. In fact, she still couldn't believe some of the things he'd taught her in bed, and she still wasn't wholly convinced that she liked to...well, experiment quite to that extent. But she never said no because she couldn't. She couldn't deny Joshua anything. He had that kind of hold on her.

She glanced at his reflection in the mirror and shivered. He was sprawled on the bed behind her, sleeping soundly, sheets tangled around his muscular legs, his bare chest exposed for her admiration. He could look so innocent at times, almost saintly, with his blond hair all messy and his blue eyes fringed with those long, golden lashes. But Crystal knew that he was anything but angelic.

A fallen angel, maybe, she thought with a shiver.

Her gaze lifted to his face, and she saw that his eyes were open now. He was watching her in the mirror. Watching her in that way he had that made her wonder at times if he could actually read her mind.

She turned. "I thought you were sleeping."

"I was." He smiled lazily. "You exhausted me."

She arched a brow. "*I* exhausted *you?*"

"That's right. You're an insatiable little so and so, but—" He patted the bed beside him. "I've got my second wind now."

She walked over to the bed, but not to join him. Instead she bent to pick up her blouse from the floor. Slipping it on, she began to do up the buttons. "I have to get back to work."

Joshua glanced at his watch. "It's nearly three. School will be out soon."

"I know, but I promised Mr. Henesey I'd come back after my doctor's appointment and help him finish a report."

Joshua grinned. "Doctor's appointment, huh? Come here and I'll give you a physical you won't soon forget."

Crystal blushed. No one but Joshua could make her blush. "I've been taking a lot of time off work lately for physicals," she murmured. "If I'm not careful, I could lose my job."

That, of course, was Joshua's cue to assure her that she didn't need a job because he would take care of her. He'd finally make an honest woman out of her. Instead he merely shrugged. "There are other jobs in town."

Crystal bit back her disappointment. She finished dressing, more determined than ever to get back to work and salvage what little faith Mr. Henesey still had in her. Because despite what Joshua said, there were *not* other jobs in town. Not decent jobs anyway, and she wasn't about to end up back at the shirt factory.

"Crystal." Suddenly the smile was gone. In its place was that dark, penetrating look he sometimes gave her. As if he could peer right into her soul, Crystal thought nervously.

"I really do have to get back," she almost pleaded.

"Come here," he demanded, and this time, when their gazes met, Crystal felt her resolve waver.

"I...can't." But she was already undoing the buttons she'd just fastened. She slipped out of her blouse and skirt, then placing one knee on the bed, she crawled toward him.

He threaded his fingers through her hair, drawing her to him, kissing her in a way that made her shudder with anticipation and some fear because she couldn't fight it. She couldn't fight *him,* even though a part of her, some leftover bit of conscience, warned her that she should.

"What have you done to me?" she whispered when he finally broke the kiss. "Why can't I say no to you?"

"Because," he murmured against her ear. "You know it wouldn't be a good idea to get on my bad side."

# Chapter Five

Marly groaned when she caught a glimpse of Deacon Cage walking into the police station late that afternoon. She knew he'd come to see her, and her first instinct was to avoid him. She didn't want to see him again, let alone talk to him. She wanted nothing to do with him or his wild suppositions, and she'd made that perfectly clear to him earlier. So what was he doing here now?

Reluctantly her gaze flickered over him. He'd changed clothes since she last saw him. He now wore dark jeans and a dark jacket that made him look even more like the mysterious stranger that he was. His hair glistened from the rain, and Marly had a sudden image of running her hand through those damp strands, stroking a thumb down the side of his face, tracing the outline of his lips with her tongue...

She blinked away the vision in horror. *My God,* she thought in shock. How could she sit there, with death still fresh on her mind, and have such an intimate fantasy about a man she barely knew? About a man she certainly didn't trust?

About a man she couldn't seem to get out of her head?

What was going on here? What had he done to her?

Marly's heart thumped erratically as she watched him speak to the cop behind the front desk. The officer turned and waved in her general vicinity, and then her heart did more than thump as Deacon started toward her.

Avoiding eye contact, Marly dropped her gaze to the open file on her desk, but she couldn't concentrate on the contents. She couldn't stop wondering what Deacon Cage was really doing in Mission Creek.

After leaving the crime scene earlier, she'd stopped by the high school to speak with Skip Manson, the job foreman for the construction company building the new gymnasium, and he'd corroborated Deacon's story—up to a point. Cage had come by the site, Skip had told her, and he had inquired about a job. But he'd also wanted to talk to the two construction workers who'd found the bodies of the teenagers on Old Cemetery Road the week before.

This revelation disturbed Marly a great deal, not only because Deacon had failed to mention it to her, but because it proved he'd been interested in the suicides before he even found out about Ricky Morales.

By all indications, he'd come to town with an agenda, and Marly was growing more suspicious of him by the moment. And she was more certain than ever that he was hiding something.

But what? And what did it have to do with her?

She glanced up reluctantly as he approached her desk. Their gazes clung for one brief moment, and Marly was struck again by how dark his eyes were. Dark...and oddly hypnotic. It took some effort to tear her gaze away.

"What are you doing here?" she blurted as she closed the file on her desk.

"We need to talk."

His voice sent a chill up her spine, but she managed to keep her tone brusque. "I'm busy."

"This won't take long. May I?" He sat down in the chair across from her desk before she could protest.

Marly glared at him. "Like I told you earlier, Mr. Cage, if you have information—real information—regarding any of these deaths, you need to talk to Chief Navarro. Otherwise, I'd appreciate it if you'd stop wasting my time."

If possible Deacon Cage's eyes grew even darker, and try as she might, Marly couldn't glance away.

"Have you told Navarro about me? About our conversation?" he asked.

"No."

"Why not?"

"Because I didn't put much credence in what you had to say," Marly said bluntly. "For all I know, you're just some crackpot who gets off trying to feed your far-fetched conspiracy theories to anyone dumb enough to listen. If I start repeating that nonsense around here, I'll be a laughingstock."

He leaned forward so suddenly, Marly pushed

back in her chair without thinking. For a moment she thought he was going to grab her.

"Believe me, this is no laughing matter. I know what you're up against here. I think you know it, too. You just won't let yourself believe it."

Marly clenched her fists in her lap. "You don't know anything about me, okay? You don't know what I believe so get a clue and leave me alone before I find a reason to throw you in lockup."

His gaze on her was grim and relentless. Completely unnerving. Gooseflesh prickled along the back of Marly's neck as she remembered her initial impression of him. He was a very dangerous man.

As if reading her mind, he leaned in even closer. So close she could smell the rain in his hair and the faint scent of peppermint that clung to his clothes. The fragrance was oddly reassuring, but the look in his eyes was not. "There's a killer in your town."

Fear churned in Marly's stomach—at what he'd said or the look in his eyes, she wasn't quite sure. She didn't want to believe him, *couldn't* believe him, but those eyes compelled her to listen just the same. "How do you explain the fact that we've found no fingerprints, no hair and fiber evidence, nothing at any of the scenes or on the bodies that would suggest foul play?"

Shadows flickered in his eyes. "He's not killing them with his hands. He's killing them with his mind."

Marly gasped. *You're crazy,* she tried to whisper, but no sound came out. All she could do was stare back at him in helpless fascination.

Obviously the man was delusional. Demented. An escapee from a psych ward no doubt. He needed help, but Marly wasn't the one to provide it. At the moment, she just wanted him gone.

"Are you familiar with the term psychokinesis?" he asked.

She frowned. "Isn't that like...bending spoons with your mind?"

He nodded. "That's part of it. But experiments in psychokinesis, mind over matter, have gone way beyond bending spoons and rolling pencils off a desk. A true psychokinetic can actually interfere with the EEG patterns of another individual's brain. He has the ability to manipulate that person's thoughts."

Marly knew he was crazy now. He had to be.

So why was she still listening to this nonsense?

Why did she suddenly feel a creeping horror up her backbone? A fist of terror closing around her heart?

It couldn't be true. It *wasn't* possible. And yet here she sat, trembling at the impossible.

"I don't believe you. No one can do that. A person can be manipulated or even brainwashed into a behavior that might otherwise be foreign to them. But what you're suggesting—"

"Goes beyond brainwashing."

Marly still couldn't tear her gaze away. "You're saying that a psychokinetic is causing these people to commit suicide by controlling their thoughts? Even if it were possible, why would he do it? What's his motive?"

Deacon shrugged. "Why does a serial killer perform such grotesque acts on his victims? Because he's fulfilling some kind of sick fantasy. Because he enjoys the manipulation of his victims. Because he wants to flaunt his power over them. In other words, his motives are complex and not fully understood by anyone but himself.''

*''Serial killer,''* Marly repeated numbly.

''Not in the familiar sense of the term,'' Deacon said. ''But you're dealing with a monster nonetheless.''

Marly drew a shaky breath. ''You must realize how crazy this all sounds.''

His gaze was still locked on hers. Marly knew she couldn't look away now if her life depended on it. ''You're looking for a man probably somewhere between the ages of thirty and forty, but he could be older. He has a military background, but he won't talk about it. He may even keep it a secret.'' Deacon paused. ''Do you know anyone like that, Marly?''

She knew a lot of people who fit that description, but she wasn't about to admit it to Deacon Cage. Not until she learned more about him and what his true agenda might be. ''Why do I get the feeling you're playing me for some kind of fool here?'' she asked angrily.

He almost smiled at that. ''If I thought you were a fool, I wouldn't be here.''

''Why *are* you here?'' Marly insisted. ''What is it you expect me to do with this...story of yours?''

''It's simple.'' He rose and stood over her desk.

"When the time comes, I expect you to do the right thing." Then he turned and strode toward the front of the station.

THE FIRST THING MARLY DID when she got home from work was strip off all her clothes and climb into the shower. She stood under the spray for a very long time, scrubbing her skin and hair time after time until she was certain no trace of that gruesome scent remained.

She wished she could wash away the bloody images as well, but that wasn't to be. She hadn't been able to get the crime scene out of her mind all day, nor could she forget Deacon Cage's enigmatic visit to the police station. *"He doesn't kill with his hands. He kills with his mind."*

A killer with supernatural powers? A man with a military background who could manipulate his victims' thoughts? Who could compel them to commit suicide?

Marly shivered even though the water was still hot.

The suicides were tragic, but there was nothing that sinister behind them. Certainly nothing supernatural. No one had compelled the victims to take their own lives. No one had controlled their thoughts. They'd made their choices of their own free will, for whatever reason. Just as her grandmother had years ago. And the fact that four different people had made that same choice in less than two weeks didn't prove anything. It happened that way sometimes. One suicide triggered another. It was like a chain reaction, Marly had read.

No one could manipulate thoughts. No one could kill with his mind. Deacon Cage was either delusional or a man with a scheme, and Marly hadn't figured out which yet. But she would. First thing the next morning, she'd have a background check run on him, and if anything suspect turned up in his file, she'd find a way to arrest him or run him out of town. If his wild story got out, Marly could only imagine the panic that a rumor about a serial killer would cause, let alone one with supernatural powers.

Stepping out of the shower, she vigorously toweled herself dry, then pulled on a pair of jeans and a T-shirt. She headed into the kitchen and opened the refrigerator, studying the contents even though she knew she wouldn't be able to eat. Not yet. Not until her stomach settled a bit.

Her gaze lit on a bottle of Pinot Grigio shoved to the very back. The trendy white wine had been Joshua's favorite, and Marly wasn't sure why she'd kept the bottle after their breakup. She wasn't much of a wine drinker, but she also didn't like to think of herself as the type of woman who needed to throw away or burn everything associated with a former lover in order to get him out of her system.

Deciding that a drink might help her relax, she grabbed the bottle by the neck and then slamming the refrigerator door with her foot, rummaged through a kitchen drawer for a corkscrew.

So what if this particular wine reminded her of the night Joshua proposed to her? she thought with grim resolve. Joshua Rush no longer mattered to her. He no longer had any power over her. She now knew him for the kind of man he really was. Beneath that charming and charismatic façade lurked a cold, cruel megalomaniac—a man very much like her father.

Thank God she'd found out about him in time. Even before she'd caught him with Crystal, Marly had already come to the painful realization that the relationship was doomed. Joshua was too self-centered and controlling. He'd cleverly disguised his true personality at first, but toward the end, he'd gone so far as to try and tell her what to wear, who to see, what to say.

No way would Marly ever live under anyone's thumb again. She hadn't had a choice as a child, but she certainly did as an adult. She would never allow anyone to have that kind of power over her.

Was that why she'd joined the police department? Because the gun strapped to her hip gave *her* power?

And if so, what did that say about her? Marly wondered.

Pouring a glass of wine, she walked into the living room, but before she could plop down on the sofa with her drink, the doorbell rang. She set the glass on the coffee table and went to answer it.

"Yes?" she said to the scantily dressed young woman who stood on the other side.

The woman gave her a nervous smile. "I don't know if you remember me or not. I used to live down the street from you. I'm Lisa. Lisa Potter. James and Nadine's daughter."

Marly stared at her in surprise. "Of course, I remember you. I was your baby-sitter when you were just this high.'' She measured the air at her waist. But Lisa had certainly changed since then, Marly thought, as she took in the young woman's skintight blue jeans and midriff-baring top. A belly-button ring sparkled in the fading light, and lip gloss glistened on a wide, sensuous mouth.

Lisa seemed to relax a bit. ''I used to ride my bike past your house every day hoping to catch a glimpse of your brother. I had the biggest crush on him.''

''Yeah, there was a lot of that going around,'' Marly said. ''So what are you doing back in Mission Creek? I heard you'd moved to Dallas a few years ago.'' In fact, she'd heard that Lisa was dancing in a strip club in one of the seedier sections of town, but Marly had no idea whether or not it was true. The woman certainly had the body for it.

''I did, but I'm back here now. My boyfriend has an apartment in this complex. I saw you drive up a little while ago. I was wondering…if you had a few minutes to talk?''

Marly had no idea what the woman might want, but she shrugged and stepped back. ''Sure. Come on in.''

Lisa followed Marly inside, then gazed around at the rather stark decor. The only thing of value in the whole apartment was the sofa Marly had purchased from an upscale design store in San Antonio. She'd blown a hefty portion of her savings on that one item of furniture because black leather was about as far removed from the French country elegance of her parents' home as she could get.

"Can I offer you something to drink?" she asked Lisa. "A glass of wine?"

"No, I'm good. Besides, I can't stay long."

Marly motioned toward the sofa. "Have a seat then." When they were both settled, she said, "So what did you want to talk to me about?"

The woman's nervousness came back. She wiped her hands down the sides of her tight jeans. "You're a cop now, right? I've seen you in your uniform."

"I'm a deputy, yes."

"That's what I thought." She clasped her fingers in her lap. "I don't know if you realize this or not, but Amber Tyson was my cousin."

"I'd forgotten about that," Marly said in surprise. "This must be a really hard time for you and your family."

Lisa nodded. "Aunt Ruby's taking it really hard. I feel bad, too, but Amber and I weren't that close. I'm a few years older so we didn't hang out or anything. And I've been away for a long time..." She trailed off, then suddenly leaned forward. "That's why I'm here. Amber and I *weren't* close. I barely even knew her. But she came to see me the day before she died. Just showed up at my apartment out of the blue."

She had Marly's undivided attention now. "What did she want?"

Lisa lifted her shoulders. "It was really weird. Like I said, we barely knew each other, and we didn't have much in common. Amber was one of the good girls, you know? Made straight As in school. Always looked and acted as if she was on her way to Sunday school. You know the type.''

*All too well.*

''That's why I was so surprised when she came to see me. Aunt Ruby would've had a fit if she'd known.'' Lisa gave a self-deprecating laugh. ''I'm kind of the black sheep of the family.''

''What did Amber say?'' Marly pressed.

Lisa frowned, as if she was still puzzled by her cousin's visit. ''She wanted to borrow an outfit. Something that would make her look older and more sophisticated. Sexy. Those were her exact words. It really freaked me out to hear her talk like that because I still thought of her as a little kid.''

''Did she tell you why she wanted the outfit?''

''Not really. But I got the impression she was trying to impress someone.''

''David?''

''I don't think so. He was the one who brought her over to my place that day, and Amber made a point of telling me they were just friends.''

''Maybe she was just too embarrassed to admit that he was her boyfriend,'' Marly suggested. ''Especially if her parents didn't approve of the relationship.''

Lisa shook her head. ''I don't think it was him. I think it was someone older. Why else would she want to look more sophisticated?''

Marly hesitated. ''She didn't mention a name?''

''No. But I think it may have been one of her teachers.''

''Why do you think that?''

Lisa shrugged. ''Because girls get crushes on cute teachers all the time, right? I had one myself.''

Marly thought about that for a moment. ''Did you get the impression that this other person returned her feelings?''

''I don't know. But I can tell you this.'' Lisa leaned forward once more, her eyes dark with concern. ''Amber wasn't suicidal that day. Just the opposite. She was happy and excited, like she had a big secret.''

''Did she say anything else?''

''No. I gave her the outfit and then she left.'' Lisa glanced at her watch. ''Look, I have to go. I'm sorry to dump all this in your lap and run, but I didn't know what else to do. I couldn't go to Aunt Ruby with it. And when I tried to tell Chief Navarro, he just blew me off.''

''Wait a minute,'' Marly said sharply. ''You told Navarro about Amber's visit? When?''

''A couple of days ago. I knew all that Romeo and Juliet stuff they were writing about Amber and David in the papers was bogus so I went down to the police station to clear it up. But when I told Navarro, he said it wasn't important. It didn't change anything, and to start a rumor about Amber and some older guy would just, you know, hurt Aunt Ruby. And I guess he has a point, but…it's been eating at me, you know? Bothering me. I can't help but think that it *is* important.''

Marly sat in silence for a moment, trying to digest everything that Lisa had told her. Why hadn't Navarro mentioned his visit from Lisa? Why hadn't he noted the conversation in the case file? He was usually meticulous about such things.

Marly got up and walked Lisa to the door. "Can I ask you something?"

The young woman turned to face her. "Sure."

"Why did you come to me?"

Lisa looked unsure for a moment, then she smiled. "When I saw you today, I remembered how nice you always were to me. And I remembered that you were really smart, like Amber. I don't know how to explain it..." She trailed off. "I guess I figured you'd know what to do."

If only that were true, Marly thought, as she watched the young woman walk away.

Twilight had fallen by the time Marly pulled off Highway Seven onto Old Cemetery Road. The rain had stopped, and a few stars twinkled in the dusky half light. Marly wanted to believe those stars were an omen that the worst of the storm was over, but she couldn't fight off a growing sense of impending doom.

What if Lisa was right? What if Amber had been involved with an older man? Wouldn't that mean that the police, as well as the media, had completely misjudged the motivation behind the double suicide? And if they'd been wrong about that, what else might they have missed?

Marly didn't want to believe that Navarro had deliberately suppressed evidence or a potential lead, but why had he failed to make note of his conversation with Lisa in the case file? Why hadn't he asked her for a statement? Was he really trying to protect Amber's family?

Navarro had never struck Marly as the sentimental type, certainly not where any of his investigations were concerned. He'd always been a by-the-book cop, so why had he slipped up now?

Was it possible that *he* was the older man Amber had been interested in? The older man that she'd wanted to look sexy and sophisticated for? It wasn't such a far-fetched notion. Half the women in town had been in love with Navarro at one time or another.

But even if he was the one, it didn't mean he'd done anything wrong, Marly reasoned. It didn't mean he was responsible for Amber's suicide. But it might explain why he hadn't taken a formal statement from Lisa Potter. And it might also call into question his involvement in the investigation. Could he really remain objective if he'd known Amber's suicide was in part motivated by her infatuation with him?

Marly knew she was reaching. Making way too many assumptions and overlooking the obvious— the other suicides. But almost any explanation was preferable to Deacon Cage's insistence that the victims had been compelled to suicide by someone with sinister intent. A serial killer. A man who could take a life with his mind. A psychokinetic, he'd called it.

Marly's hands tightened on the steering wheel as she pulled off the main street onto a narrow service road and parked her baby SUV near a thicket. Once she turned off her headlights, the countryside was darker than she'd anticipated. She glanced around uneasily at her surroundings.

Old Cemetery Road had once led directly into Fort Stanton, but the entrance was barricaded now and the entire property surrounded by a metal fence topped with razor wire. Signs posted at intervals warned that trespassers would be prosecuted to the fullest extent of the law.

Which, of course, was an irresistible lure to local kids. Marly knew that some of them had recently found a way inside. She'd heard stories in town about their nocturnal explorations of the base, about discovering underground bunkers filled with computer and electronic equipment and guards who roamed the premises dressed all in black and armed with futuristic-looking weaponry.

Marly figured the stories were at best gross exaggerations. Fort Stanton had been closed for years. While some equipment had undoubtedly been left behind, she seriously doubted anything of value remained, and the military personnel she'd seen passing through town on their way to the abandoned base had all been dressed in fatigues. There was nothing sinister about their appearance or their actions.

Still, she had to admit there was something about the army base that made her uneasy. She could never explain it, but even on the rare occasions when she'd accompanied her father to his headquarters, she'd sensed something ominous about the place.

Unlike most kids who found themselves in such an environment, she hadn't been interested in the uniforms, or the guns, or the heavy artillery. Instead of using the opportunity to explore, Marly had cowered in her father's office, certain that something terrible awaited her outside his walls.

As she grew older, she came to realize that it wasn't the base or the soldiers or the equipment that frightened her. It was her father. In her mind, she couldn't separate the two.

Colonel Wesley Jessop had spent the last ten years of his career at Fort Stanton, and when the base closed, he'd retired rather than accept a new assignment.

The arrangement had always seemed a bit strange to Marly. Rather than being dragged from post to post like other army brats, she and her brother, Sam, had lived most of their lives in Mission Creek. She supposed she should be grateful for the stability, but somehow gratitude was an emotion that didn't spring immediately to mind when she thought of her childhood.

Grabbing a flashlight from the glove box, Marly climbed out of the vehicle and closed the door. If there were guards around tonight, she hoped they wouldn't spot her or her car. If she were picked up, the mention of her father's name would probably be enough to obtain her release, but then she'd be indebted to him. And being indebted to her father was a fate far worse than spending a night in the brig.

Making her way across the main road, Marly jumped a ditch and headed into the area the locals still referred to as Mission Creek Cemetery. Back in the 1940s, the graves had been exhumed and relocated to a lot on the other side of town when the base's expansion threatened to overtake them. But even though the graves were gone, everyone still considered the ground hallowed, and Marly tried to tread respectfully. If any spirits lingered, she didn't want to offend them.

Turning on her flashlight, she carefully picked her way across the marshy ground. She honestly didn't know what she hoped to find. Certainly not a smoking gun, so to speak, that had been overlooked in the daylight search five days ago when David and Amber's bodies had been found. But there might be something.

A twig snapped somewhere behind her, and Marly whirled, unsure whether she'd actually heard the sound or if her imagination was getting the better of her.

"Is someone there?" she called out nervously.

No one answered.

She started to call out again, but didn't particularly want to call attention to herself. For all she knew, there could be guards patrolling nearby. But she was trapped in a catch-22 because she also didn't want to be shot on sight for trespassing. Technically the cemetery had never become part of Fort Stanton, but Marly was afraid an armed guard with an itchy trigger finger might not make the distinction.

"I'm Deputy Marly Jessop with the Mission Creek Police Department! If someone's there, please show yourself!"

Still no answer. No sound at all except for the steady drip of rainwater from the trees.

Marly wished she had her gun with her, but she never carried her weapon off duty. Besides, she'd had no reason to believe she was in any danger coming out here. She still had no reason to believe that.

So why was her heart pounding so hard inside her chest? Why was her breathing shallow and irregular?

She was scared, that's why, and suddenly Marly wondered if Deacon Cage was so crazy after all. Maybe he was right. Maybe there was a killer in Mission Creek, and maybe that killer was somewhere nearby, watching her...

Marly let out a shaky laugh to relieve the tension. Now she really was letting her imagination run wild. Next thing she knew, she would be doing something totally against her will because the killer had taken control of her mind—

Another noise froze her in her tracks. This time Marly recognized it instantly. It was the sound of her own voice. She had started to sing, softly, mindlessly, a tune that had tormented her sleep for years.

*Gloomy Sunday...Gloomy Sunday...Gloomy Sunday...*

## Chapter Six

The rain came down in a steady drizzle the next day as Deacon drove over to Sam Jessop's house to see the garage apartment he'd heard Nona Ferris mention. He'd called first thing that morning to set up an appointment, and Sam had agreed to meet him there after school.

Deacon's first impression on meeting the man face to face was that he didn't look anything like his sister. But as Sam led the way up the outside stairs to the apartment, Deacon caught flashes of Marly in his profile, in the stubborn set of his jaw and chin.

He wondered briefly what she would say when she found out he intended to rent her brother's apartment or how she would react if she knew he considered Sam Jessop a viable suspect even though Camille had yet to turn up anything incriminating on either Sam or Navarro. Or even Fort Stanton, for that matter.

But Deacon had learned a long time ago to listen to his gut. His instincts had told him that Marly was the one who could help him find the killer, and they were telling him now that Sam Jessop was a man with a secret.

Sam turned at the top of the stairs, his gaze dark and wary. "The place is pretty small. Hope you're not claustrophobic."

The place was tiny, in fact, but Deacon liked what he saw. Oak floors, beamed ceilings, and tall windows that would let in plenty of light if the rain ever let up.

The furnishings, however, left a lot to be desired. The maroon sofa was in good condition, but the style was from a different era, as were the other odds and ends of furniture and knickknacks.

"What do you think?"

Deacon walked into the apartment and glanced around. "Not bad. It may be just what I'm looking for. Assuming, of course, the rent is reasonable." Not that it really mattered. Deacon wasn't overly concerned about the money. He was more interested in being able to keep tabs on Sam Jessop's comings and goings.

Sam named a figure, and Deacon nodded without a quibble.

"So how long did you say you're in town for?" The question was casually asked, but Deacon sensed there was more than curiosity behind it.

"I didn't say. My plans are up in the air at the moment."

Sam nodded, but he didn't look particularly satisfied by the answer. "How did you happen to hear about the apartment anyway?"

"Someone in town mentioned that you had a place for rent." Deacon shrugged. "I was in the market so I decided to come by and have a look."

"Even though you don't know how long you'll be staying in town? A little unusual to rent an apartment under those circumstances, isn't it?"

"I won't skip town in the middle of the night, if that's what you're worried about," Deacon assured him. "In fact, I'll pay you three months rent plus the security deposit up-front."

Sam lifted a brow. "Just like that? You don't want to see the other rooms?"

"No need to. I like what I've seen so far. Besides, I don't want someone coming along and renting it out from under me."

Sam gave a wry chuckle. "You obviously haven't been in town long. We don't exactly have a booming real estate market here."

"Do we have a deal then?"

"We have a deal." Sam offered his hand, and the two men shook. "When do you want to move in?"

"The sooner the better," Deacon said. "Tonight if possible."

Sam looked surprised. "That soon? I've done some painting and cleaning in here, but the place could still use a good airing." He ran his hand over the top of a table, as if inspecting the surface for dust.

Deacon watched his future landlord move about the apartment. Even if Nona Ferris hadn't mentioned that Sam Jessop had been in the service, Deacon would have known by the way the man carried himself, by the way he walked, even in the way he spoke. Deacon suspected Sam had spent several years in the military, and the discipline, as well as his experiences, was now deeply ingrained in his psyche.

Sam glanced up. "Do you have family in the area, Mr. Cage?"

"Deacon. And no. I don't have anyone in town. Actually, I came here to look up an old acquaintance, and I liked what I saw so I decided to stay awhile."

"Kind of an odd place to settle down for a man without connections," Sam observed. "There's not a lot to do around here."

"Luckily I don't require much in the way of entertainment."

Sam started to say something else, but his cell phone rang, and with a murmured apology, he extracted the unit from his pocket and walked over to the window, keeping his voice low so that Deacon couldn't overhear the brief conversation. When he turned back around, he was frowning. "Sorry to cut this short, but I have to go." He strode to the door. "You can stay as long as you want, just lock up when you leave. Oh." He tossed Deacon a key. "You'll need this to get back in."

"What about the money?"

"Bring it over to the house when you come back. And if you need help moving in your stuff, just let me know."

"Thanks, I will."

A second later, he heard Sam's footsteps clatter down the outside stairway.

Deacon walked over to the window and pulled back the shade. He watched as Sam hurried through the drizzle to the safety of the covered patio attached to the main house. But instead of going inside, he paused to glance up at the garage apartment.

Deacon stepped back from the window, but he could still see Sam on the patio below him. There was an odd expression on the man's face, one Deacon didn't know how to interpret. But it set off warning bells inside him just the same.

After a moment, Sam Jessop turned and disappeared inside the house.

MARLY HAD ONLY BEEN TO HER grandmother's house a few times since Sam bought the place from their parents, but not because she didn't like to spend time with her brother. The two of them had grown quite close since he'd left the service and moved back to Mission Creek.

But the house held too many bad memories. Gruesome memories. Memories that had caused Marly nightmares for years, although, truth be told, she'd never felt that much sorrow at her grandmother's passing. Isabel Jessop had been an embittered old woman whose only pleasure in life had been derived by inflicting misery on others, especially Marly's mother.

Isabel had been tyrannical, egotistical and, more often than not, downright cruel, but to Marly's dismay and her mother's credit, Andrea Jessop had never said a word against her mother-in-law. In fact, Andrea had been the only one to worry when the old lady hadn't shown up for church on that fateful morning.

The rest of that day was burned into Marly's memory. Even now she could still see her grandmother's feet swinging in a stray breeze from somewhere inside the house. Marly could still picture the lilac dress, the missing shoe, and the glitter of those diamond earrings. And she could still hear that music.

Drawing a deep breath, Marly pressed her thumb to the doorbell. When the door finally opened, she was momentarily taken aback by the strange face she saw through the screen. Then she recognized him and blurted, "What are you doing here?"

Max Perry gave her a quizzical look. He was the guidance counselor at the local high school and had been working closely with the police department since the two students' deaths. "Sam invited me to dinner. Will you be joining us?" he queried politely.

"Uh, no. I just came by to see him for a minute. Is he here?"

"He's gone over to the garage apartment to make sure everything is in order for his new tenant." Max motioned her inside. "Come on out to the kitchen. He should be back soon."

As he led her down the narrow hallway, Marly couldn't help noticing how perfectly at ease he seemed in her brother's house. She, on the other hand, had to fight the urge to glance over her shoulder to make sure she wasn't leaving muddy footprints.

Out in the kitchen, Max walked over to one of the glass-fronted cupboards and took down two cups. "Coffee? I just made it."

"No, thanks," Marly murmured, struck again by how at home he seemed in her brother's kitchen.

"Oh, that's right." He poured himself a cup. "Sam mentioned that you're not a coffee drinker. You're probably better off for it. I'm sure I drink too much of the stuff."

"I didn't realize you and my brother were such good friends," Marly remarked curiously.

He shrugged. "Well, we work together, you know. And with all the turmoil at school lately, we've all more or less bonded."

Carrying his cup over to the table, he motioned her to a chair across from him. "I heard about Ricky Morales. They said on the radio that the cause of death hasn't yet been determined, but naturally there's speculation that it's another suicide."

Marly watched him lift the cup to his lips. He had nice hands, she noticed. His nails were neatly clipped, filed, and buffed—in much better shape than hers. Self-consciously she folded her hands in her lap. "We'll know more after we get the autopsy results."

Max nodded. "If it does turn out to be suicide, then it's more important than ever that we start a suicide hotline."

Marly knew that Max had been discussing the feasibility of a hotline with Navarro. She thought it was a good idea. "I understand you've also been holding some after-school meetings where kids can come and talk about what happened. How do you think they're handling the situation?"

Max ran a hand through his wavy hair. "It's hard to tell at this point. These suicides are troubling for everyone. I'm thinking about opening up the meetings to the whole community. The students aren't the only ones who need support at a time like this."

Marly couldn't have agreed more. "Have you ever seen anything like this, Max?"

He toyed with his coffee cup. "No, but I've read about it. Sociologists refer to it as cluster suicides."

Marly paused. "Can I ask you something?"

He flashed her a charming smile, one that made him look ten years younger. "You can ask me anything."

"Even if it sounds…totally off the wall?"

He grinned. "Now I'm intrigued."

"Do you know anything about mind control?" she asked tentatively.

The question clearly startled him.

"I guess what I'm asking…" She paused and bit her bottom lip. "This may sound crazy, but I guess what I'm asking is if it's possible for these suicides to be caused…by someone else."

He shook his head. "I'm not sure I follow."

She slid a hand through her damp hair. "Is it possible, in your opinion, for someone to manipulate another person's thoughts to the extent that they can cause that person to do something he or she wouldn't ordinarily do?"

Curiosity flickered in his eyes. "You mean like brainwashing?"

She nodded. "I guess. I know it happens in cults."

He thought about it for a moment. "It's true that charismatic cult leaders have been known to be extremely persuasive. Charles Manson was even able to induce his devotees to perpetrate heinous murders. And I suppose you could even argue that women who remain with abusive husbands are suffering from a form of mind control. So, yes, I guess it is possible, but I don't think it very likely in this case. The victims don't seem to be connected, and even in incidences of cluster suicides there's usually a common thread. Age. Location. Or in the case of the Midwest farmers back in the 1980s, their occupation. We don't have anything like that here, do we? Unless I'm missing something?"

Before Marly could question him further, the back door opened, and she was almost relieved to have their conversation interrupted. She had a feeling she'd been on the verge of blurting out everything Deacon Cage had told her, and the last thing she wanted was to start rumors. The town was edgy enough.

"Well, this is a nice surprise," her brother said. He came over and gave her a quick hug. "You're staying for dinner, I hope."

"I was just about to try to persuade her." Max got up to top off his cup. He didn't come back to the table, Marly noticed, but stood leaning against the counter, one foot crossed over the other as he sipped his coffee.

Marly rose, too. "Thanks for the offer, but I can't stay. I just came by to see if I could look through some of Grandmother's things."

"Don't tell me you want a keepsake," Sam teased her. "Something to remember our loving grandmother by."

Marly gave him a wry smile. "Look who's talking. I'd say you have the ultimate keepsake. How you stand living here is beyond me."

Sam shrugged. "I've always liked this place. It's a great old house. Has good bones." He glanced around with pride. "Besides, I'll take great pleasure in exorcising Isabel's ghost from each and every room."

Marly suppressed a shudder. She didn't think that would happen no matter how much he renovated and redecorated.

"Are you looking for anything specific?" Sam asked her.

"Her old 78s," Marly said. "She had quite a collection the best I remember."

"Yeah, I've been meaning to look through all that stuff myself." Sam opened a cupboard and took down a jar of spaghetti sauce. "All her records are still in her bedroom, I think. The old phonograph should be up there as well. You want me to come up and take a look with you?"

"No, thanks, I can manage."

His gaze flickered, and Marly knew he was remembering, just as she was, the last time she'd been in their grandmother's bedroom. "Sure you don't need some help?"

"I'll be fine. You two enjoy your dinner."

Marly exited the kitchen, and was halfway up the stairs when she thought of something else she wanted to ask her brother. She backtracked down the hall to the kitchen, then paused in the doorway, her question frozen on her lips.

Sam had joined Max at the counter, and the two of them stood with their backs to Marly. They were staring out the window, speaking in low tones, and Max's hand was on Sam's sleeve.

The intimacy of the gesture sent a shock wave through Marly. Quietly she backed away from the door, then turned and hurried down the hallway toward the staircase.

# *Chapter Seven*

Pausing at the top of the stairs, Marly switched on the hall light, then glanced around, trying to reorient herself to the second floor. Even as a child, she'd rarely been in this part of the house. The upstairs had been off limits. When the family had made their biweekly visits, Isabel had allowed Marly and Sam only into certain rooms. Most of the time they had been relegated to the front porch or the backyard where they could be seen and not heard.

But every once in a while, Marly and Sam would sneak away to explore. Sam loved the attic with all its hidden booty, but Marly had always been drawn to her grandmother's bedroom. The beautiful hand-blown perfume bottles and pots of face cream she kept on her dressing table was an irresistible lure to an adolescent girl who wasn't even allowed to wear clear fingernail polish.

Marly's father had once caught her sampling her grandmother's lipstick, and she could still remember the icy rage in his voice as he'd ordered her to scrub her face and then come downstairs to face the music. She'd descended slowly, in great dread, never so terrified of his temper.

Her grandmother had stood beside him at the bottom of the stairs, her aging face twisted in smug self-righteousness. "See there, Wesley," she crowed in triumph. "I've told you over and over those kids are out of control. They're nothing but ill-bred, disrespectful little heathens, and you can thank your misguided wife for their abominable behavior. Perhaps if she would have spent a little more time with them instead of with that fancy shrink in San Antonio, the two of them might have learned some manners."

"Don't worry," her father said coldly. "I'll handle this." He took Marly's arm and hauled her across the foyer and out the front door to the porch.

He didn't kneel so that he could talk to her face to face, but had remained towering over her, his face rigid with fury. "Your grandmother is right. You're a disgrace, Marlene Louise, and it's high time you were taught a lesson about respecting other people's property."

He'd never hit Marly before, but there was something in his eyes that day, something...out of control.

Sam must have sensed it, too, because he charged up the porch steps, his fists clenched, his eyes just as fiery as their father's. "Leave her alone!"

Their father whirled in surprise, caught off guard by Sam's outburst. And when he started toward him, Sam refused to back down. He stood his ground, even when their father grabbed him, dragged him into the yard, took off his belt, and laid into him.

Marly stood crying on the front porch as she watched, but Sam didn't shed a single tear. And when their father was finished, her brother straightened, looked him right in the eye, and saluted.

The gesture infuriated their father even more, but from that day forward, it seemed to Marly that he treated Sam with a bit more respect. And from that day forward, Sam had been Marly's hero.

The memory faded, replaced by a more recent image—Max Perry's hand upon her brother's arm. Marly filed that memory away, too. She didn't have time to think about it now, but later she would. Later she would take it out and analyze it, turn it this way and that and try to figure out what it might mean, but for now she needed to concentrate on the business at hand.

She entered her grandmother's bedroom with trepidation. The room was just as she remembered. Neat and orderly. Furnished with dark, heavy furniture. A white chenille bedspread covered the bed and lace curtains hung at the windows.

The room was pleasant enough, Marly supposed, except for the bad memories. The moment she'd turned on the light, her gaze had been drawn to the ceiling beams, and she had a feeling that the dark spirit of her grandmother still hovered somewhere nearby.

Shivering, she crossed the room to the old phonograph that had once graced the front parlor. It now rested atop a burled walnut console, which housed her grandmother's prized collection of 78s.

Marly knelt and began thumbing through the

covers. She didn't know the artist's name so she had to read through all the song titles. When she finished, she went back and rechecked, but "Gloomy Sunday" wasn't among any of the recordings.

Was it possible the police had confiscated the recording when they'd searched the house after her grandmother's death? Several other items had been taken during the course of the investigation, and Marly had no idea if any of them had ever been returned. For all she knew, the record might still be locked up somewhere in the evidence room at the police station.

Dusting her hands, she rose and walked over to the window to stare out. A light was on in the garage apartment, and she remembered that Max Perry had said Sam had a new tenant.

As she watched the rain, her thoughts turned once again to Sam and his dinner guest, and she couldn't help wondering if there was a secret her brother had been keeping all these years.

"I'M LOOKING FOR SAM," Deacon said a little while later when a man he'd never seen before answered his knock at the back door.

"You must be the new tenant." The man stuck out his hand. "I'm Max Perry, a friend of Sam's."

"Deacon Cage."

From somewhere inside the kitchen, he heard his new landlord call out a greeting. "Come on in, Deacon."

Max Perry stepped aside to allow him to enter. Then he walked over and leaned against a counter, watching Deacon with dark, curious eyes. He was as tall as Sam, but lankier, and his tweed jacket and black-rimmed glasses gave him a distinguished, intellectual air.

Sam stood at the stove, stirring a pot of something that smelled delicious. Deacon hadn't eaten anything since breakfast, and the delectable aroma made him suddenly aware of his empty stomach.

Sam turned from the stove. "I'm making spaghetti. Nothing fancy. Just a few spices added to store–bought sauce. But you're more than welcome to join us."

The offer was tempting, and Deacon might have taken him up on it if he hadn't noticed the impatient look the invitation drew from Max Perry.

"Thanks, but I still have some unpacking to do." He held up an envelope. "I've brought you the rent money."

Sam nodded toward the counter. "Just put it there."

"You don't want to check it?"

"I know where to find you if you're short." He seemed different tonight, Deacon thought. Friendlier and less guarded. "If you won't stay for dinner, how about a quick drink? Max just opened a bottle of wine, but I'm having a beer."

"A beer sounds good," Deacon agreed.

"Max, would you do the honors?" Sam turned back to the simmering pot.

"Certainly." Max extracted a cold beer from the refrigerator. "Mug or bottle?"

"Bottle is fine." Deacon accepted the drink and twisted off the cap.

"So what brings you to Mission Creek?" Max asked as he poured himself a glass of wine.

"He came to town to look up an old acquaintance," Sam supplied before Deacon had a chance to answer.

Max lifted an eyebrow. "Well, I'm afraid you've picked a lousy time to visit. The weather is atrocious, and now with all these suicides…" He trailed off. "You've heard about them, I suppose."

Sam turned with a scowl. "Damn it, Max, can we go one night without talking about the suicides? That's all anyone at school ever talks about these days. I'd like to have one conversation that doesn't revolve around death and rain."

"I only brought it up because Marly and I were talking about it earlier," Max explained. "She has an interesting theory about cults."

"Cults?" Sam scowled. "What the hell are you talking about?"

Max sipped his wine. "Cults as in mind control. Brainwashing."

"You're joking, right? A cult in Mission Creek? That's a good one." But Sam's expression was anything but amused.

"It might not be as far-fetched as you think," Deacon murmured.

Max glanced at him curiously. "Except for the fact that the victims appear to have no connection."

"Maybe the connection just hasn't been made yet," Deacon said.

Sam's amicable mood had vanished. His expression was downright glum now. "What kind of connection could there be?"

"Yes," Marly said from the doorway. "That's what I'd like to know."

The moment Deacon's gaze met hers, his stomach tightened in awareness. She wore faded jeans tonight and a soft yellow sweater that brought out the gold in her eyes. She even had on lipstick. The delicate pink sheen made her lips look full and lush and indescribably sexy.

Marly wasn't a particularly pretty woman, but there was something about her, a kind of budding sexuality that seemed on the verge of full bloom. And in the throes of passion, she would be beautiful, Deacon thought.

"Marly," Sam said. "I'd like you to meet Deacon Cage. He's rented the garage apartment. This is my sister, Marly."

"We've met." Marly came slowly into the room, an angry glint in her eyes. "So you are planning to stay in town then."

"For the time being." Deacon gave her an amused glance. "No law against that, is there?"

Her mouth tightened as she tucked her short hair behind her ears. "Let's get back to what you were talking about when I came in. If you've discovered a connection in all these deaths, I'd be very interested in hearing about it."

"There's one connection I'm sure you've already thought of," Deacon said.

They all stared at him expectantly.

"Two students, an ex-teacher and a man employed on campus."

Marly's expression was skeptical. "You think the high school is the connection?"

"It's *a* connection," Deacon said. "Whether or not it played a factor in any of the deaths, I can't say."

"But Gracie Abbot retired years ago," Marly pointed out.

"She still occasionally substituted," Sam said reluctantly. "Although she wasn't used very often. Not to speak ill of the dead, but she wasn't well-liked by either the students or the faculty."

"Too much of a busybody," Max muttered.

A hissing sound from the stove brought Sam around with a curse. "Damn, I've let the sauce burn."

Deacon set aside his beer and straightened. "I'd better shove off and let you get to your dinner."

"Sure you won't stay?" Sam asked.

"No, thanks. I need to get back to my unpacking."

Sam turned to his sister. "Marly?"

"I have to go, too. I'll walk you out," she said to Deacon.

Once they were outside, she stopped on the patio and glanced back at the door.

Deacon peered at her in the darkness. "Anything wrong?"

She shook her head. "No, I was just wondering about something. But it doesn't matter. I'm more interested in finding out how you came to rent my brother's apartment."

He shrugged. "I heard someone mention yesterday that he had a place for rent."

"And the fact that the apartment belongs to my brother is just a coincidence?" she asked doubtfully.

"What else could it be?"

"I don't know," she said. "You tell me."

"Marly." He started to place his hands on her shoulders, but thought better of it. "Your brother had an apartment for lease, and I happened to be looking for a place. It's as simple as that."

"Why do I get the impression that nothing involving you is simple?" Her eyes gleamed in the rainy darkness. "I don't know why you're here, but I have my suspicions. My guess is that you're a reporter sniffing around for a story or you're a private investigator hired by one of the families to dig up something they can use in a lawsuit. Or else..."

He lifted a questioning brow.

She let out a breath. "Or else you're just flat out crazy."

"I'm not crazy," he assured her. "And the only reason I'm here is to help you."

"That's what you keep telling me," Marly said angrily. "But what you don't seem to understand is that I don't need or want your help. There is no killer in Mission Creek."

"You're wrong, Marly. Dead wrong."

He saw her shiver in the darkness. "Then prove it."

"You want proof?" His voice held a note of challenge. "Come up to my apartment and I'll give you what you need."

THAT WAS THE OLDEST LINE in the book, and Marly shot him a disgusted look, but her heart began to hammer.

"Are you scared to come up to my apartment?"

Yes, she thought. She was very afraid. But she shook her head in denial.

"Then come on up," he urged softly. "I have something I want to show you."

Marly knew she should resist, but instead she found herself nodding in agreement—although she had no idea why—and followed him out into the rain.

They climbed the steps together, and Deacon stood back to allow her to enter the apartment first.

He'd left a light on earlier and Marly glanced around, recognizing the odds and ends of furniture that had once belonged to her grandmother.

"I'm sorry I can't offer you something to drink." Deacon closed the door behind them. "I haven't made it to the store, yet."

"That's fine. This isn't a social call," Marly reminded him.

"At least let me take your jacket."

Marly realized she was dripping on the rug. She slipped out of the windbreaker and handed it to him. "Sorry."

"No problem. Would you like a towel?"

"No, don't bother." She wrapped her arms around her middle. "Let's just get this over with."

If her brusqueness irritated him, he didn't let on. He walked over to the table and picked up a folder. "Take a look at this."

Reluctantly Marly joined him. Opening the folder, she quickly scanned through the contents, thinking at first the dozens of newspaper clippings about a series of suicides had been snipped from the local paper. Then she realized the dateline was almost two years old.

She glanced up in confusion. "I don't understand."

"What's happening in Mission Creek has happened before," Deacon said grimly. "Two years ago there was a series of unusual suicides in Glynnis, Oklahoma. Seven people took their own lives in a four-week period."

"So?" Marly closed the folder and handed it back to him. "That doesn't prove anything. Suicides happen from time to time, even in small communities. Even within a single neighborhood. Max Perry said it was known as cluster suicides."

"This isn't the same thing," Deacon said. "Cluster suicides have a catalyst or a common bond among the victims. The suicides in Glynnis appeared unrelated. The victims were from disparate backgrounds, age groups, careers. No connection was ever found."

"But that still doesn't prove it was anything other than suicide," Marly insisted.

"It wasn't suicide. It was murder."

"Are you saying the suicides in Glynnis and the ones here are somehow related?" she asked incredulously. "Are you saying the same person is responsible?"

He shook his head. "It isn't the same person. But they have the same ability."

"They kill with their minds." Marly felt ridiculous even saying it. "I'm still not buying it."

"Then I guess I'll just have to prove it to you." His voice made Marly shiver with awareness, and she wondered how wise she'd been to come up here with him. Crazy or not, he was a very attractive man, and she was…she was a cop, was what she was. She could handle Deacon Cage.

He laid the folder aside and glanced down at her. "I told you before that the man you're looking for has a military background. He was once part of a black special ops team connected to an underground organization known as the Montauk Project. It was run by a group of scientists and paramilitary personnel whose goal was to create an army of secret warriors—super soldiers—with psionic abilities who would stop at nothing to accomplish their mission."

"Psionic abilities as in psychokinesis?"

"Among others, yes."

Marly almost laughed. He had to be pulling her leg. "And you expect me to believe that? Secret warriors? Super soldiers? Come on." When he didn't smile, her own amusement turned to amazement. "You can't be serious. Look, if you tell me we're dealing with a psychopath so cunning he can make his kills look like suicide—I might be willing to hear you out. If you tell me he's so clever and meticulous that he doesn't leave behind even one speck of DNA or trace evidence—you'd probably get my attention. But this crazy X-Files explanation is ridiculous. I don't know what your agenda is, but you've wasted my time bringing me up here.''

She turned to leave, but Deacon caught her arm. ''Wait a minute, Marly. I told you I could prove it, remember?''

The way he said her name sent a fresh tremor through Marly. His voice was very seductive, his eyes hypnotic. She tried to look away, but couldn't.

He was standing very close to her now, and Marly caught her breath as she gazed up at him. She wanted to back away, wanted to turn and run, but she couldn't. She was paralyzed, unable to move, unable to do anything but tremble with dread. With anticipation.

Lifting a hand, he trailed a finger along her jawline, and she still couldn't move. He skimmed her throat, the V-neckline of her sweater, and Marly offered not so much as a whimper.

Cupping a hand around the back of her neck, he drew her to him, and she came—not willingly but without will. Without choice.

She wanted to close her eyes and break the spell he'd cast over her, but she couldn't even do that. Instead she moistened her lips and parted them for his kiss. And when it finally happened, her breath rushed out on a gasp. Her knees went weak with shock.

Her eyes drifted closed then, but the spell remained. If anything she became more deeply enthralled as he pressed his mouth against hers, forcing her lips to open fully. And then his tongue invaded.

Marly trembled all over, shivered as if she were freezing, but her body was in flames. She was no stranger to a man's mouth, a man's hands, a man's body. But she'd never been so totally consumed by a man as she was now. She'd never been in danger of losing control as she was at that moment. She didn't recognize herself. Didn't recognize the moans emanating from her own throat.

She flattened a hand against his chest, but not to push him away. Instead she slid her palm downward, along the sleek muscles of his abdomen, and lower still, to press against the front of his jeans. And now it was he who groaned against her mouth, he who seemed on the verge of losing control.

His hands moved inside her sweater, finding and cupping her breasts, and Marly arched into him.

She was so lost in the moment that she didn't immediately realize when it was over. But suddenly Deacon was no longer kissing her. His hands left her breasts to straighten her sweater. Then he pulled away from her.

And Marly had never felt so bereft in her life. So utterly betrayed.

SHE GLANCED UP AT HIM, her eyes clouded with confusion and lingering desire. He'd been right, Deacon thought. In the throes of passion, Marly Jessop was a beautiful woman.

As she stood frozen in place, the bewilderment in her eyes slowly turned to disbelief. Then to fear.

And finally to horror as it dawned on her what had happened.

Deacon had seen that look before.

He put out a hand to her, but she jerked away. "Don't touch me." She began backing toward the door. "What did you do to me?" she whispered on a ragged breath.

"Marly—"

"Don't say my name. Don't come near me. Don't even look at me." She was at the door now, and she paused with her hand on the knob. "I don't know who you are," she said through gritted teeth. "I don't know *what* you are, but stay away from me. Do you hear me? Stay the hell away from me."

MARLY DASHED THROUGH THE RAIN to her car, jerked open the door, and jumped inside. Starting the engine, she careened away from the curb, her tires spinning dangerously on the wet pavement. She warned herself to slow down, to concentrate on her driving before she ended up in a ditch, but she couldn't think of anything but Deacon Cage. Couldn't forget what had almost happened between them. What he had *made* happen.

But that wasn't possible, she told herself. He couldn't force her to do anything against her will. She must have wanted it. A part of her must have invited it.

She clutched the steering wheel with trembling hands. Through the rain-streaked windshield, she could see intermittent flashes of lightning where a fresh storm gathered on the horizon. Marly drove straight toward it. Drove without looking back. Drove through the night as if the nastiest demons in hell were chasing her.

Her heart still pounding, she wheeled into a parking space near her building, then ran through the rain to her apartment. Locking herself inside, she collapsed against the door and squeezed her eyes closed, trying to block the memories. But she couldn't forget. How could she, when she could still taste Deacon Cage's mouth on her lips, still feel his hands on her breasts? When her whole body still churned with her desire for him?

Stumbling across the room in the dark, she lay down on her sofa, cradling a pillow in her arms as she drew her knees up to her chest.

''What's happening to me?'' she whispered.

Marly was no virgin, but she realized now that was a mere technicality. Deacon Cage had opened up a whole new world for her, one she could never have imagined.

And it scared her. Frightened her as nothing ever had. Not even her worst nightmares.

Rolling onto her back, she watched the flicker of lightning through the window. The storm drew steadily closer, but Marly knew that whatever bad weather the night might bring would pale in comparison to the tempest raging inside her.

A silent storm, she now realized, that had been building for years.

DEACON FROWNED AS HE WATCHED Marly's car tear away from the curb, and he caught his breath when she momentarily skidded out of control. Only when he lost sight of her taillights did he realize his hands were clenched tightly at his sides. He relaxed them, but it didn't ease the tension inside him.

He should never have let her go racing off into the rain as upset as she was, but under the circumstances, there wasn't much else he could have done. He'd already gone too far with her. He'd frightened her so badly he might not be able to repair the damage. He might never gain her trust.

But he hadn't been able to help himself, and that was the scariest part of all. He'd made her want him in order to prove a point, but in proving that point, he'd found himself wanting *her*. He'd almost done the unthinkable. The unforgivable. He'd almost lost control of the situation, and that was a very dangerous thing.

He started to turn from the window, but in a flash of lightning, he saw something move in the yard below him.

Deacon watched the spot for several long moments until another flicker of lightning convinced him that his eyes were playing tricks on him. No one was there.

But as he continued to stare into the rainy darkness, he felt it. A gentle probing. A tentative exploration inside his head. In the split second before Deacon became fully aware of the danger, an invisible tentacle had almost penetrated his mind's defenses.

He'd let down his guard for too long. He'd become distracted by his attraction to Marly. That couldn't happen again.

Because Deacon knew, with a dreaded certainty, that the killer was here. Close by. And he had just thrown down the gauntlet.

## Chapter Eight

Marly knocked on Navarro's door the next morning, then stuck her head inside his office. "You wanted to see me?"

He waved her in. "Come in, Deputy, and close the door."

Max Perry was seated across from Navarro's desk, and he rose when Marly entered. But the third person in the room was the one who made her stomach sink. Joshua Rush leaned against the wall, arms folded, as he gave her an insolent once-over.

With his dark blond hair and baby-blue eyes, he had the clean-cut, all-American good-looks that made people want to trust him. His magnetism was undeniable, but what most people didn't see—or chose to ignore—was the cruelty behind that dazzling smile.

Marly glanced nervously at Navarro, feeling as if she were about to be ambushed.

He gestured to a second chair across from his desk. "Have a seat."

Marly complied, folding her hands in her lap and

keeping her eyes focused straight ahead. But she could feel Joshua's gaze on her, and reluctantly, she stole a glance in his direction. He gave her a smile, that slow, charismatic smile that had once fooled her so utterly. The same smile that now had the power to chill her blood.

She glanced back at Navarro. "What's going on, sir?"

"Max here tells me the two of you talked at some length last evening about the recent deaths in Mission Creek."

She nodded. "We had a discussion, yes." Had Max mentioned her interest in cults and mind control? Was that what this meeting was all about? Did Navarro think she'd gone off the deep end?

After the incident in Deacon Cage's apartment the night before, Marly wasn't so sure she could put up much of an argument in her defense. She still got cold chills when she thought about her loss of control.

"He tells me that you have an interest in the suicide hotline that he's proposed."

"Well, yes," Marly said, breathing a little easier. "I've always thought it was a good idea."

"I'm glad to hear that." Navarro leaned back in his chair. "I'd like you to assist Max in any way you can to get it up and running. We've already arranged for a special number from the phone company, and for now, we'll use the conference room as headquarters. The next step is making sure word gets out to the community. That's where you come in."

"What is it you want me to do?" Marly asked.

"For one thing, we'll need to get flyers printed and passed out. You can help with that. Max has also been conducting a series of after-school meetings that he wants to open up to the public. He's holding the first one tonight in the high school auditorium, and I'd like you there as the police department's representative. We have to make sure the community knows that we're deeply concerned about these deaths and fully committed to finding some answers." Navarro paused, his gaze meeting Marly's. "Any questions so far?"

Yes, Marly thought. She had plenty of questions. She wanted to believe Navarro was giving her this assignment because he had complete faith in her, but somehow she wasn't convinced that was his true motivation. She couldn't help wondering if he'd somehow found out about her visit from Lisa Potter and if he was assigning Marly busywork just to distract her.

"Max has also arranged for the two of you to be interviewed on the Phil Garner radio program this afternoon," Navarro was saying.

*"Interviewed?"* The mere thought of having to answer questions on a live broadcast made Marly's palms sweat. "I don't know that I'm the best person—"

"Relax," Max murmured. "I'll do most of the talking."

Marly flashed him a grateful smile, then her gaze shifted back to Joshua. What was his part in all this? Had he somehow convinced Navarro to give her this assignment because he considered it more appropriate to her gender and capabilities than, say, investigative work? Or even handing out traffic citations? He'd always harbored certain expectations for his future wife, and on the day she'd called it quits, Marly had told him exactly what he could do with those expectations.

Their breakup hadn't been amicable, and Marly had no wish to interact with her former fiancé now, even on police business. She'd successfully avoided him for months, and now here they were, in the same room, only a few feet apart, and he was smiling that smile.

*He's up to something,* Marly thought with an unexpected shiver.

"You're probably wondering what I'm doing here." His blue gaze taunted her.

"We're calling on the leaders of all the area churches to get involved," Navarro explained. "We asked Reverend Rush to attend this initial meeting because his church has been the most affected by these suicides."

Joshua's face was the perfect mask of concern and sorrow. "It's been a very trying time for our congregation, as you can imagine. You may remember, Marly, that David and Amber were very involved in our youth group, and Miss Gracie not only sang in the choir—and did so beautifully, I might add—but was also one of our most devoted Bible schoolteachers." His eyes moistened right on cue. "Naturally I'm anxious to do whatever I can to help the community cope with these tragedies."

Plus, the suicides were bad for business, Marly thought cynically. If people lost faith in him, the attendance would drop at the Glorious Way Church and so would the Sunday collections.

The meeting went on for several more minutes, and then finally Navarro drew it to a close. Marly got up to follow Max and Joshua out, but before she could exit, Navarro called her back in.

He gestured toward the chair she'd just vacated. "I get the feeling you're not exactly thrilled about your new assignment."

His comment caught her off guard. "It's not that," she said, dodging. "It's just...I'm not sure I'm the right person for the job. I haven't even been working for the police department all that long, and I certainly don't have any public relations experience. To tell you the truth, I'm not even much of a people person."

"This is new territory for all of us," Navarro said. "No one in the department has any real PR experience that I'm aware of it. But you do have a college education, and you know how to talk to people without stepping on any toes. That's more than I can say for most of my deputies."

"But my degree is in education," Marly pointed out.

"All the more reason why you're qualified for this assignment. When you were teaching, you had to be able to deal with difficult people in difficult situations, didn't you?"

Yes, Marly thought. Which was why she'd only

lasted a year in the classroom. Aloud she said, "I'll do my best."

He nodded. "That's all I ask." When Marly started to rise, he said, "Just one more thing." He leaned forward, folding his arms on his desk. His eyes were very intense, Marly noticed, and she had a strange feeling that he was somehow testing her. "I heard Deacon Cage came by here to see you the other day."

Marly's backbone tingled at the mere mention of his name. "Yes, he did."

Navarro toyed with a pen on his desk. "What did he want?"

"He has a theory about the suicides," Marly said hesitantly.

"So does everyone in town," Navarro muttered. "What's his?"

Marly wasn't sure how much she wanted to tell Navarro, or anyone else, about her conversations with Deacon Cage. Last night was still too fresh in her mind. "He said something about the suicides...not being suicides."

Navarro glanced up. "He said what?"

Marly shrugged. "I know it sounds crazy. In fact, I thought he was crazy at first. Some nutcase who'd heard about the suicides on the news and decided to come down here and try to interject himself into the investigation. Now I think he's here for another reason."

Navarro's gaze narrowed. "Such as?"

"I think he's either a tabloid reporter trying to create a new angle on the story in order to sell more papers, or else he's been hired by one of the families to dig up something that could be used in a lawsuit, maybe by discrediting the police department.''

Navarro seemed to mull that over for a moment. ''Have you run a background check on him?''

''Yes, but so far nothing's turned up.''

''Well, keep digging,'' Navarro said grimly. ''Whatever scam he's trying to pull, he seems to have marked you as the target. See what you can find out about him, but watch yourself. For all we know, that guy could be dangerous.''

*Tell me something I don't know,* Marly thought as she rose and exited Navarro's office.

WHEN SHE CAME OUT OF THE station a little while later, Joshua was waiting to see her. He called out her name, but Marly ignored him. Hurrying down the steps after her, he grabbed her elbow to stop her.

She whirled and jerked her arm from his grasp. ''What do you think you're doing?''

He raised both hands, as if to prove he wasn't a threat. ''I just want to talk to you, that's all.''

''We don't have anything to talk about.''

His expression turned remorseful. ''You're wrong, Marly. You can't sweep everything that happened between us under a rug and hope it'll somehow go away. It won't. Not until we sort things out.''

Marly gave a bitter laugh. ''I think everything was pretty much sorted out in your office that day. I don't need to rehash it. That chapter of my life is over. I don't even think about it anymore.''

"Liar." He smiled knowingly, making Marly's blood run cold and then hot with fury. The man's ego knew no bounds.

"You have the nerve to call *me* a liar?" she demanded. "Your whole life is nothing but a lie."

"Now, Marly," he said, in that condescending tone she'd come to despise. "It's time to let go of the bitterness. It's not becoming, and besides, if we're going to be working together—"

"Let's get one thing straight," she cut in. "You and I are not going to be working together. Not if I have anything to say about it."

He gave her his wide-eyed, innocent stare. "Didn't you hear what Navarro just said? He wants all the church leaders to be involved in his community outreach program. And since you'll be acting as liaison for the police department, we'll be spending a lot of time together. Which, I have to admit, I'm looking forward to. It'll give us a chance to straighten out some of our differences, and who knows? We may even be able to rekindle our romance."

"When hell freezes over," Marly said through gritted teeth.

He just laughed. "Didn't your mother ever tell you it's not wise to burn bridges?"

"Some bridges are best blown to smithereens," Marly said coldly. "You were always so concerned about your image. I wonder what would happen to your reputation if your congregation knew about your affair with Crystal Bishop while you were still engaged to me."

Suddenly the innocence was gone and the true Joshua Rush was revealed by the gleam of anger in his eyes, by the cruel set of his mouth. He grabbed Marly's arms, catching her by surprise, and hauled her against him. "Who would believe you? It would be your word against mine, and everyone in town knows how pathetic you are. Here you are, twenty-eight years old, and you can't even muster enough courage to crawl out from under your father's shadow. He says jump, you still say how high."

Before Marly could pull away from him, a male voice said from behind her, "Is everything okay here?"

She recognized that voice and groaned inwardly. The last thing she wanted was to be rescued by Deacon Cage.

Joshua's smile was angelic as he released her. Every trace of anger had miraculously vanished. Even the lock of blond hair that fell across his forehead made him look boyish and charming. "I'm sorry," he said, extending his hand toward Deacon. "I don't believe we've met. I'm Joshua Rush. Reverend Rush."

Deacon ignored the outstretched hand as his gaze swept over Marly. "You okay?"

"Of course." With an effort, she tried to keep her demeanor cool and professional. She didn't want his assistance, nor did she need it. She could handle Joshua Rush. She'd done it before and she could do it again. "Was there something you needed?" she asked pointedly.

"I'd like to have a word with you." Deacon glanced toward Joshua. "In private."

Joshua frowned, not accustomed to being dismissed. "Do you want me to hang around for a bit?" he asked Marly.

Oh, this was great. Just great. Joshua wanted to protect her from Deacon, Deacon wanted to protect her from Joshua, and Marly didn't trust either man as far as she could throw him.

"No," she said to Joshua. "I don't need you to hang around. You and I are finished." There was no mistaking her meaning, and Joshua's mask slipped for one brief second, revealing his anger and annoyance, before the smile settled firmly back in place.

"Well, in that case, I should probably get back to my office. I'll see you soon." He bent, brushing his lips against hers before Marly could protest. "I can hardly wait," he whispered.

Suppressing a shudder, Marly waited until he was out of earshot before she turned back to Deacon. And as their gazes met, she felt her nerve endings jump to attention. She suddenly remembered in graphic detail every tingle, every touch, every nuance of *his* kiss. She remembered the way she'd kissed him back, the way she'd touched him—

Marly tore her gaze from his as her face went hot with embarrassment.

"We need to talk about last night," he murmured.

She lifted her chin. "No, we don't. The only thing that needs to be said about last night is that it won't happen again."

"It wasn't your fault, Marly."

She clenched her fists at her sides. "If you're trying to tell me you somehow manipulated me into…doing what I did, then you're wrong. No one can make me do anything I don't want to do. You can't control my thoughts. You can't get inside my head." She forced herself to take a deep breath and lower her voice. "Last night just happened. It was a mistake. Let's leave it at that."

"Do you really believe that, Marly? Is that the way you normally respond to a first kiss?"

She had never responded to *any* kiss that way in her life. But it wasn't because Deacon Cage had controlled her mind and manipulated her thoughts. No one could do that. Not her father. Not Joshua Rush. *No one.*

For some reason, Marly had been vulnerable last night. Needy. Perhaps even a little sexually frustrated. But Deacon Cage hadn't *made* her respond to him.

"I meant what I said last night. I want you to stay away from me."

"Why?"

The moment she glanced at him, his dark gaze captured hers. His eyes held her imprisoned, enthralled, and Marly couldn't seem to look away no matter how hard she tried.

"If you don't think I manipulated your response last night, then why are you afraid of me?" he challenged.

*Isn't that obvious?* Marly wanted to scream. She wasn't terrified that he'd made her respond. She was terrified that he hadn't.

PHIL GARNER WAS A DIMINUTIVE man whose placid, bookish demeanor was at complete odds with his rich baritone radio voice and his gregarious, some-times abrasive, on-air personality. He was something of an institution in Mission Creek, having been on the air for as long as Marly could remember. He was not only the owner and general manager of KBRT, but also director of programming, news-reader, talk show host and disc jockey.

He'd agreed to devote the last thirty minutes of the *Phil Garner Show* that day to Max Perry and Marly, and had, in deference to the serious subject matter, toned down his brusque interview style. Nevertheless, he asked probing and insightful ques-tions, which Max handled with professional aplomb.

Marly had to admit that both men were thor-oughly prepared, and she felt more than a little inadequate sitting between them in the soundproof booth. It was a relief when the on-air sign went off and she was able to remove her headset. While Max gathered up his notes, Marly turned to Phil. "Do you have a minute or two? I'd like to talk to you."

Max glanced at her curiously. "Shall I wait for you?"

"No, you go on. That is, if Phil can spare me a moment?"

He glanced at his watch. "I've got a little time. Walk me back to my office."

They said their goodbyes to Max, then the two of them headed down the hallway.

"So what's up?" Phil asked as he opened his

office door and turned on the light. He motioned Marly toward a chair across from his desk.

When they were both settled, she said, "Are you familiar with a song called 'Gloomy Sunday?'"

He glanced up. "Any particular reason why you're asking?"

"My grandmother used to play it," she said hesitantly. "I've always been curious about it."

His gaze turned speculative. "It doesn't have anything to do with what's been going on around here?"

"What do you mean?"

He shrugged. "'Gloomy Sunday' is called the suicide song."

Marly stared at him in shock. "Why?"

"You really didn't know?" He sat back in his chair and folded his arms across his chest. "There's quite a story behind it. I don't know how much is true and how much is urban legend, but 'Gloomy Sunday' drew a lot of notoriety in Europe back in the 1930s when it was connected to a rash of suicides."

Marly's nerve endings tingled. "Connected how?"

"Supposedly the lyrics were quoted in a suicide note a man wrote before jumping out a seven-story window. Another man shot himself after hearing the song played in a nightclub. The stories go on and on, but my favorite is the errand boy in Rome who overheard a beggar humming the tune. The boy parked his cycle, gave the beggar all his money, and then threw himself off a bridge."

Marly suddenly had a strange feeling in the pit of her stomach. She couldn't help wondering if her grandmother had known about these stories, as well.

"I've got the Billie Holliday version here at the station if you'd care to listen to it," Phil said. "As a matter of fact, I had a request for it just the other day."

Marly glanced up sharply. "Do you know who made the request? And when?"

"I can find out. At least as to the 'when' part." Phil swiveled around to the computer on his credenza. "We keep a log of all the requests made and played so that we don't end up repeating the same songs over and over." He scrolled down the screen, then paused. "Here it is. The request came in last Sunday, the thirteenth, just after noon. The caller specifically asked that 'Gloomy Sunday' be played at one o'clock that same afternoon."

"Do you know the caller's identity?"

"Nah, sometimes they give a name, but most requests are anonymous. My producer is the one who screens the calls. You can talk to her if you like, but I doubt she'll remember. We have an all-day request line on Sundays, and we get a lot of calls for all kinds of music. She jots down the name of the song and the time and date it goes out on the air, and then later we enter it into the log. Like I said, we don't like to repeat ourselves."

Marly nodded, but her mind reeled with the information he'd given her. Sunday, the thirteenth, was the day of the first suicide. At one o'clock in the afternoon, Gracie Abbott would have just been arriving home from church and pulling into her garage.

CRYSTAL BISHOP LOWERED herself into the tub of hot water and sighed as she sank to her neck in bubbles. She was running late and should have settled for a quick shower, but a leisurely soak was just too tempting. Besides, she'd waited for Joshua plenty of times. She'd waited almost a whole year for him to call her after he and Marly broke up. He could damn well wait for her this time.

Still, she knew he'd be in a foul mood when she finally did show up at his place. He had little patience for tardiness, except his own, of course. It seemed to Crystal that he had little patience for anything she did these days. She didn't want to admit it, but she was smart enough to read the signs.

It was obvious Joshua had someone else on the side. Someone Crystal would never have suspected, but she'd seen them together with her very own eyes that morning.

She'd just happened to be driving by, and there they were, standing pressed up against one another, gazing into each other's eyes.

Crystal had been replaying that scene in her head all day, trying to make sense of it. Trying to convince herself it wasn't what she thought. It couldn't be. Not with the way Marly felt about Joshua.

From somewhere inside the house, Crystal heard something that sounded like a door clicking shut. She lay perfectly still in the bubbles, listening for the sound again, but when she didn't hear anything, she decided it had either been her imagination or one of her neighbors slamming a car door—

No, there it was again. But a different sound this time, like someone rummaging through a drawer.

Crystal's heart leaped to her throat. Someone was in her house, going through her things.

Normally, she wouldn't have been so quick to jump to conclusions, but after everything that had being going on in town…old lady Abbott…those kids. And then poor Ricky…

She eased herself out of the tub and holding a towel to her chest, padded across the linoleum to close and lock the door. Then she glanced around. What was she going to do? There wasn't a phone in the bathroom and her cell phone was in her purse. Even if she could somehow force open the window over the tub, she wasn't sure she could slither through it.

Maybe she should be cool and wait it out, Crystal decided. It was probably a couple of stupid kids looking to score some drug money. They'd find her purse, take what little cash she had, then split. As long as she didn't cause any trouble, they wouldn't hurt her—

The knob on the bathroom door jiggled, and Crystal gasped, clutching the towel to her chest. Shivering uncontrollably, she watched the knob turn back and forth and then, in horror, she saw the lock rotate to the unlocked position.

But that wasn't possible. Not unless someone had somehow managed to jimmy the lock from the other side—

The door swung open and Crystal screamed and jumped back. The floor was wet where she'd stood dripping, and her feet flew out from under her. With a thunderous crash, she fell back against the tub, cracking the back of her skull on the porcelain.

Groaning, she put her hand to the back of her head and felt something wet. Trying to shake off the dizziness, she scrambled toward the door, but someone blocked her path.

Her breath came in tiny little gasps as she gazed up in confusion. "Wh-what are you doing here?"

Something fell on the wet floor beside her, and Crystal stared at it in horror.

And then, in slow motion, she reached for the knife.

# Chapter Nine

Deacon detected panic on more than a few faces in the crowded auditorium that night. Most of those in attendance were parents of teenagers who'd gone to school with David Shelley and Amber Tyson, and they'd come to the meeting desperately hoping to hear something that could help them prevent such a tragedy in their own family.

But they had no idea what they were up against, Deacon thought as he leaned a shoulder against the wall and watched the proceedings get underway. They reminded him of lambs being led to the slaughter.

He scanned the auditorium, wondering if the killer was out there somewhere, well hidden among family and friends.

Shifting his focus to the stage, he let his gaze linger on Marly. She still wore her uniform, and he wondered why he hadn't noticed before how well it suited her body. For a small woman, she was surprisingly curvy. Curvy and sensuous and dangerously sexy. Dangerous for him, at least.

What was it about her that had gotten to him? She wasn't beautiful or particularly sophisticated. She was just an inexperienced, small-town cop who packed a wallop the likes of which he hadn't experienced in years.

Deacon hadn't been able to get her out of his head since she'd fled his apartment the night before. He'd even dreamed about her last night. Dreamed about her mouth, open and eager beneath his, her body pliant and willing against his. He'd awakened early this morning aroused and frustrated and more than a little unsettled by the ease with which she'd gotten under his skin. With the way he'd let down his guard with her.

Unable to fall back asleep, he'd stood at the window, watching another rainy dawn break over the horizon as he'd vowed to keep the situation with Marly firmly under control.

But in spite of his resolve, he hadn't been able to stop thinking about her all day, even after her brush-off that morning. And now he couldn't keep his eyes off her.

Her demeanor on stage was that of a woman who wasn't particularly comfortable in the limelight, and for some reason, that made her even more attractive to Deacon.

She answered questions when they were directly addressed to her, but otherwise she seemed content to hover in the background and allow Max Perry to occupy center stage. Deacon hadn't been overly impressed with the man the evening before, but tonight he had to admit that Perry conducted the meeting with compassion, insight and a good deal of common sense.

Deacon watched for a few more minutes, then slipped away. Outside, he located Marly's car, and then glancing around, melted into the shadows to wait for her.

When she came out of the auditorium half an hour later, it had started to rain again. She glanced skyward, grimaced, then made a run for her car. By the time she got across the parking lot, Deacon was waiting by her door.

Marly stopped short. Ignoring the rain, she glared up at him. "What are you doing here?"

"I came to see you."

"I thought I made myself crystal clear this morning," she said coolly. "Now please move away from my car."

Deacon stood his ground. "I was out of line last night and I want to apologize."

She swiped her damp hair out of her face. "That isn't necessary. I told you this morning, I don't blame you for what happened. It was just as much my fault as it was yours. All I want to do is forget about it."

"But can you?"

She gave a heavy sigh. "Not if you persist in pestering me about it. Look," she said impatiently. "I accept your apology, okay? Case closed."

Deacon nodded. "I appreciate that. But I still say we got off on the wrong foot. I'd like to make it up to you."

She rolled her eyes. "You just don't give up, do you?"

"I can't. Not when lives are at stake."

"Well, then you can relax," she said with an edge of sarcasm. "I saw Ricky Morales's autopsy report with my own two eyes today. Cause of death was a self-inflicted gunshot wound. It was tragic, just like all the others were. But it wasn't murder."

Deacon cocked his head slightly as he gazed down at her. "How can you be so sure?"

"Because of the evidence. Or maybe I should say, the lack of evidence. And contrary to what you seem to think, you didn't prove anything to me last night."

That sounded like a challenge to Deacon, and he was tempted to prove to her right then and there what he could do. It would be so easy to make her want him again. All he had to do was look into her eyes and make the connection. Manipulate her mind and her emotions until all she could think about was having him. Until her feelings became so intense they would overwhelm her.

Sex would be incredible between them. He could make it so. But then afterward when she knew, when she realized what he had done, she would hate him. She would never trust him again. Might never trust anyone, and that wouldn't be right because a woman like Marly needed love, even if she didn't know it yet.

"Have dinner with me tonight," he said impulsively.

Marly looked shocked by the invitation. "I...can't. I already have plans."

Deacon felt a pang of unreasonable jealousy and wanted to ask her to cancel them. Instead he said with a shrug, "Coffee then."

"I don't drink coffee."

"Hot chocolate, tea, Coke. There's a café down the block."

She nodded. "The Red Duck. It's been there forever."

"Will you meet me there?"

She started to say no. Deacon could tell it was on the tip of her tongue, but then suddenly she changed her mind and nodded.

If he was lucky, she wouldn't figure out why until much later.

MARLY ARRIVED AT THE café first, and rather than waiting for Deacon, she hurried inside, brushing raindrops from her shoulders and hair. A bored waitress showed her to a red vinyl booth by the window and once Deacon arrived, poured him a cup of coffee. A few minutes later, she returned with Marly's hot chocolate.

The rain was coming down harder now, beating a steady rhythm against the plate glass window. Nights like this always got to Marly. Made her feel lonely and bereft.

Ignoring the hollow feeling inside her chest, she lifted her cup, letting the steam from the hot chocolate ward off her chill. "How did you know where to find me tonight?" she asked curiously.

"I heard about the meeting on the radio this afternoon."

She made a face. "You heard that? Did I come off as lame as I think I did?"

"You were fine."

"Yeah, I'll bet." Marly sighed. "It was Navarro's idea. I guess he figured he'd rather have me on the radio than running around town with a gun. Can't say as I much blame him for that," she muttered. "I haven't exactly found my niche in the police department yet."

"You seemed in control of the situation at Ricky Morales's house the other day," Deacon pointed out.

Marly glanced up in surprise. "Did I?" She felt unaccountably pleased by his observation.

He took a tentative sip of his coffee, eyeing her over the rim of his cup. "So what made you want to be a cop?"

She shrugged. "I never really *wanted* to be a cop. I needed a job and there was an opening at the police department."

"What did you do before that?"

"I worked at a church."

His brows rose. "Reverend Rush's church?"

Marly's jaw hardened. "Yeah, as a matter of fact."

Deacon set aside his coffee. "This morning when I saw the two of you outside the police station I got the impression that you know each other fairly well."

"I guess you could say that." Marly spooned a

bite of whipped cream from her hot chocolate. "Joshua and I were once engaged."

He didn't say anything for a moment, but Marly could tell that she'd surprised him. Maybe even shocked him. "What happened?" he finally asked. Then, "Never mind. That's none of my business."

"No, it's not," Marly agreed. "It's no one's business, but that doesn't stop people around here from talking about it. Some of them have made it pretty clear they think I'm an idiot for letting a man like Joshua slip through my fingers."

"I would have thought it the other way around," Deacon said.

Marly's stomach fluttered with awareness. Okay, maybe she didn't exactly trust the man, or trust herself with him, but he did have a way with words, she had to admit. "You only say that because you don't know me very well," she accused.

"No. I say that because I've met Reverend Rush."

Marly couldn't help grinning. "What, you weren't bowled over by all that boyish charm? That movie star charisma?" She took another bite of the whipped cream. "You should see how his congregation treats him. They practically worship *him* on Sundays, and he loves it. He revels in the adoration, not to mention the generous contributions from his most faithful devotees."

"I take it you don't exactly have regrets about the breakup," Deacon said.

"Let's just say, I spent the first eighteen years of

my life with a man like Joshua Rush. I wasn't about to spend the rest of my life with another.''

Their gazes met across the table, and Deacon nodded, as if he understood completely what she was saying. It was a momentary bonding that caught Marly by surprise. And took her breath away.

Her heart began to pound as she realized they were completely alone in the café. Even the waitress had somehow disappeared.

She thought again about the kiss they'd shared, and before she could help herself, her gaze dropped to Deacon's lips. They were full and well-shaped. Sexy and kissable. What would he do, she wondered, if she leaned across the table and planted one on him? Would he pull away?

Not if last night was any indication. Marly had a sudden image of him hauling her across the table and kissing her back until she had no will of her own. Until she lived for nothing else but the feel of his lips on hers, the whisper of his warm breath against her neck, the pressure of his hands on her breasts...

She tore her gaze away and stared out at the rain.

After a moment, Deacon said, ''Tell me about your father.''

Marly frowned. ''Why do you want to know about him?''

''Because I have a feeling that to know you I have to know about him.''

She stabbed at the whipped cream with her spoon. ''There really isn't much to tell. He's a domineering megalomaniac who tried to control every aspect of my life, just like he does my mother's. I've watched him browbeat and bully her for years. She can't so much as plan a menu without his okay. He tells her how to dress, how to wear her hair, even what she can eat for dinner. If she gains a pound, he ridicules her until she drops it. If she buys a dress without his permission, he makes her take it back. If he could control her every thought, he would. But he can't do that. At least...he couldn't with me.'' Her voice hardened. ''He could make me wear clothes that I hated and eat food that I despised, but he couldn't control my mind. No one can.'' Her gaze dared him to dispute her.

When he didn't, she softened a little. ''You know the saddest part of all? My mother has never known anything else. Her father was just like him. In fact, my father was my grandfather's protégé when he was first stationed at Fort Stanton. When my grandfather was sent to the Pentagon, my father took over as base commander. He's a lot older than my mother, and I always wondered if he married someone so young just so that he could try and mold her into the kind of wife he always wanted.''

''Is that the reason you became a cop?'' Deacon asked. ''So you could be in control?''

Marly was surprised by his insight. ''Partly, I guess. And partly because I knew my father wouldn't approve. Men like him have certain expectations for women, and being a cop isn't one of them.''

''What about your brother?'' Deacon asked carefully. ''Does he take after your father?''

"Sam? You've met him. He's nothing like my father."

"But he followed in your father's footsteps, didn't he? I heard he was in the army for a while."

Marly's gaze narrowed in suspicion. "Why are you so interested in Sam?"

Deacon lifted his coffee cup. "He's my landlord. And he also happens to be your brother."

"Why are you so interested in *me?*" Marly demanded.

*Because you're fascinating,* Deacon wanted to tell her. "Because I need your help. And you need mine."

"To find a killer who doesn't exist." She closed her eyes and shook her head. "I don't know what I'm even doing here," she muttered.

Deacon leaned toward her. "Because you know I'm right. You know he's out there somewhere."

"I'm just supposed to take your word for that?" Marly let out a long breath. "You waltz into town making all kinds of outrageous claims, and I'm just supposed to blindly trust you? I don't know anything about you."

"You know enough."

"I know *nothing*," she said angrily.

He sat back and studied her for a moment. "That would help? To know something about me?"

She shrugged. "It couldn't hurt."

"What is it you want to know?" Deacon asked reluctantly.

"I don't know." Marly tucked her hair behind her

ears. "Since you're so interested in my family, why don't you tell me something about yours?"

"I don't have any family."

"No one?"

He shrugged. "It's better that way. If you don't have a family, no one can use them against you."

"Use them against you? You sound like you're in the mafia," Marly said dryly.

"Not the mafia. But I do deal with some pretty dangerous people in my line of work. People who aren't exactly happy with what I do now," he said cryptically.

"And what exactly do you do?"

Again he hesitated, as if debating on how much he should tell her. How much she would believe. "I work for an organization that tracks killers."

Marly caught her breath. "You mean like…the FBI?" she asked inanely.

"No, not like the FBI." His gaze lifted. "Do you remember what I told you last night about the Montauk Project?"

"You said something about a black special ops team," Marly said. "Super soldiers with—what did you call it? Psionic abilities?"

"Five years ago, a team of these soldiers boarded a submarine for a clandestine rendezvous in the North Atlantic. The mission was so highly classified the men were to be briefed only minutes before they reached their destination. But there was an explosion on board before the drop. The submarine crashed to the bottom of the Atlantic, trapping everyone on board. By the time the rescue team arrived several days later, it was too late to save most of the crew. Six members of the special ops team were the only ones who survived the accident.''

Marly stared at him in confusion. ''What does that have to do with you? With what's happening in Mission Creek?''

''I'm getting to that.'' Deacon waited until the waitress had topped off his coffee before continuing. ''After the men recovered, they underwent rigorous debriefing sessions that included comprehensive brainwashing techniques that not only destroyed their memories of the mission, but also of the experiments they'd been subjected to, in some cases for years. They were discharged from the military as mentally unfit to serve, which meant if any of them ever talked, no one would believe them.'' He leaned toward Marly. ''The problem was...they'd been trained to kill, you see.. And some of them didn't know how to stop.''

''And that's where you come in,'' Marly said.

He nodded. ''The organization I work for has been tracking these men for years. Not just the survivors of the submarine accident, but the ones who went through similar experiments at the abandoned Montauk Air Force station on Long Island.''

''Tracking them how?'' Marly asked. ''You have a list of names?''

He shook his head. ''It's not that easy. The names of all the subjects were purged from the files when the project was abandoned. But we have other ways of finding them,'' he said ominously.

''Such as?''

"When they use them, their special abilities cause talk," he said. "We follow the rumors. And in some cases, the trail of dead bodies."

Marly suppressed a shudder. "This organization…is it connected to our government?"

"In a manner of speaking. But if you were to ask anyone in the intelligence community, they would deny its existence, just as they would deny the whole Montauk fiasco."

That sounded a little too convenient to Marly. As if he were covering his bases, making sure she had no way to check out his story. "You said the special ops team aboard that submarine was on a highly classified mission. If it was so secret, how is it you happen to know so much about it?"

"Because I was on board that submarine. I was a member of that team."

Marly glanced up, her gaze wide. "Are you saying you were…a super soldier?"

"Yes," Deacon said grimly. "I was trained to kill. And I did so with ruthless precision."

## Chapter Ten

Contrary to what Deacon had told Marly earlier, his questions about her brother were generated by far more than just casual interest. One of the darker secrets of the Montauk Project was that they'd used the children of military personnel as their test subjects. Their victims of choice were males between the ages of nine and twelve who excelled in both athletics and academics. Deacon suspected that Sam Jessop, the son of an army colonel and the grandson of a general, had been the perfect candidate.

From the front window in his apartment, Deacon watched now as Sam came out of the house, climbed into his Jeep, and backed out of the driveway. Then he waited until the vehicle's taillights were out of sight before he left the apartment and hurried down the outside stairs. He melted into the shadows of the covered patio to reconnoiter, but he didn't think he was in any danger of being detected. The patio couldn't be seen from the street, and the rain and darkness would protect him from any neighbors who happened to be glancing out their windows.

The lock on the back door was a flimsy, old-fashioned model that Deacon could easily have picked, but it wasn't necessary because Sam had left the door unfastened. It was almost like an invitation, Deacon thought uneasily.

Letting himself inside, he paused in the kitchen to get his bearings. He'd committed the furniture placement to memory two nights ago, and now he made his way unerringly across the room to the door.

Slipping silently through the darkened house, he followed the hallway to the foyer. The front parlor was to his right, the stairway to his left. He went up quickly.

The first room at the top was a bedroom. He took out a flashlight and quickly circled the area with the beam. Everything appeared clean and orderly, but the scent of old memories seemed to permeate the space. Deacon remembered what Nona Ferris had told him about Marly's grandmother that first day on the porch of Ricky Morales's house. She'd committed suicide years ago and Marly was the one who found the body.

Deacon wondered if this was the room where it had happened. He could picture Marly—small for her age and quietly intense—as she came slowly up the stairs, perhaps already sensing what she would find at the top.

A floorboard creaked somewhere in the house and Deacon whirled. He stood for a moment, listening to the dark, and then dousing the flashlight, he stole across the room to the door. Flattening himself against the wall, he eased down the hallway to the top of the stairs.

No one was there.

He started to turn away, but a subtle noise, like a pencil rolling off a desktop, caused him to freeze.

And almost instantly, he realized his mistake.

The noise had come from downstairs, but the intruder was already upstairs, using the power of his mind to create a diversion. In the split second before Deacon understood this, the killer came rushing out of the darkness toward him.

Deacon still had his back to the hallway, and before he could turn, something slammed into the back of his head. Pain exploded behind his eyes as he pitched forward, reaching blindly for the banister.

But he couldn't stop his momentum. He went crashing downward, bones and flesh bouncing off the wooden stairs until he landed at the bottom with a jarring thud. He couldn't tell how badly he was hurt because he couldn't move. He couldn't even lift his head.

But in that brief moment before everything went black, Deacon could have sworn he heard music. A monotonous tune that repeated itself over and over.

EVERY THURSDAY NIGHT, come hell or high water, Marly was expected at her parents' house for dinner. The days leading up to that dinner had become something of a ritual for her. She started thinking about it on Monday, worrying about it on Tuesday, sweating over it on Wednesday, and by Thursday afternoon, she'd be almost sick with dread.

Marly often wondered why she kept punishing herself by going. Why not just put an end to the farce once and for all? The only logical answer she'd ever been able to come up with was that she did it for her mother. As much as Marly hated those Thursday night dinners, her mother looked forward to them. It was the one night of the week when she didn't have to spend the evening alone with her husband.

As far as Marly knew, her father had never laid a hand on her mother, but he had other ways of intimidating. Other ways of tormenting. He was a cold, ruthless man with an uncanny knack for zeroing in on a person's weaknesses, including his own children.

By the time Marly rang the doorbell, she'd worked herself up into quite a state. Her palms were already clammy, her stomach tied in knots. If Mrs. Hicks, her mother's housekeeper, hadn't answered the door so promptly, Marly might actually have turned and fled back into the darkness.

But it was too late now. Mrs. Hicks ushered her into the foyer and took her raincoat and umbrella.

"Where's Mother?" Marly asked as she brushed raindrops from her hair.

"She's running a little late tonight. She asked me to tell you she'll be down shortly."

Marly was instantly worried. Her mother was never late. Her father wouldn't abide tardiness. "She isn't sick, is she?"

"She didn't mention anything about feeling under the weather." Mrs. Hicks busied herself hanging up

Marly's coat and umbrella. "Colonel Jessop is in the den if you want to go in and keep him company," she said over her shoulder.

Marly grimaced inwardly. That was pretty much the last thing she wanted to do. "I think I'll freshen up first." If she played her cards right, she could kill at least two or three minutes in the powder room before having to face her father.

She took so long touching up her hair and makeup that when she finally came out, her mother was just coming down. Marly went to greet her.

Andrea looked lovely as always. Her pale blond hair was expertly arranged in the sleek pageboy style she'd worn for years, and her stark, long-sleeve dress emphasized her narrow shoulders and tiny waist. Her makeup, as usual, was applied with a light hand. She looked classy, understated, and elegant. There was nothing in her demeanor or her attire that would raise eyebrows or cause talk. The years of being a colonel's wife—and before that, a general's daughter—had taught her well. No one could find fault with her appearance, although her husband frequently tried.

She bent and gave Marly a hug. "It's so wonderful to see you."

Marly hugged her back, feeling the sharp ridges of her mother's rib cage beneath the smooth fabric of her dress. Marly pulled back in concern. "Mrs. Hicks said you were running late. Are you okay? You're not sick, I hope."

"I'm fine, dear. I had a last-minute errand to run." She lifted a hand to Marly's cheek. "But it's sweet of you to be concerned.'' She smiled, and it suddenly hit Marly that there was something different about her mother tonight. Something subtle. Her hair and makeup were the same, but her eyes seemed to glow with an inner excitement.

Marly caught her breath. *My God,* she thought. *She really is beautiful.*

What had put that light in her mother's eyes? Marly couldn't help wondering. Surely something more than the anticipation of seeing her children at dinner.

The doorbell rang, and her mother gave her another quick squeeze. ''That'll be Sam. I'll let him in. You go on in and join your father.''

Marly would much rather have waited for Sam, but her mother gave her a nudge, urging her forward, and reluctantly Marly entered the den where her father sat reading a book. He was tall and muscular, in very good shape for a man well into his sixties. He was still the same weight as the day he'd retired from the army, and he still retained the same rigid posture and adhered to the same meticulous care of his appearance, right down to the spit and polish of his black shoes. There wasn't a speck of lint on his dark suit. There wouldn't dare be.

''Hello, Father.''

He glanced up from his book. ''Marlene.''

No one had ever called her by that name except her father and grandmother. She despised it.

His critical gaze swept over her leather skirt and black V-neck sweater. She had never been allowed to wear pants to the dinner table as a child and teenager, and for some reason Marly couldn't break the habit now. But leather was pushing it.

"You look like a streetwalker in that getup," was her father's only comment.

Her skirt was a sedate cut and length, and the neckline of her sweater didn't reveal so much as a hint of cleavage. Marly lifted her chin. "Just the look I was going for."

Her father didn't bother to respond. "There's been another suicide, I hear. Navarro must have his hands full."

"Yes, he does," Marly agreed. "As a matter of fact, he's assigned me to act as liaison for the police depart—"

"Liaison? I'm surprised you even know what the word means."

Marly felt her face go hot with anger, but she held her temper. She wanted to keep the evening as pleasant as possible for her mother's sake. "I'll be working with Max Perry, the high school counselor, and various church leaders in the community to establish a suicide hotline and organize a series of meetings…" Her voice trailed off. She was wasting her breath. Her father had gone back to his book. "Congratulations, Marly. Well done, Marly. I knew you could do it, Marly," she muttered.

He glanced up. "What?"

"Nothing. Here's Mother." She rose in relief as her mother and Sam walked into the room.

He put away his book then and gave Sam the same disapproving glare he'd accorded Marly. But there was one big difference. Sam no longer cared.

He hadn't bothered to dress for dinner. Or, to be more precise, he had. The faded jeans and black turtleneck had been a deliberate wardrobe choice, Marly was quite certain. Jeans were outlawed in the Jessop household, and a row between father and son was already starting to brew. Marly could feel it. An uneasy chill rode up her backbone.

"Well," her mother said with forced cheeriness. "Isn't this nice? All of us here together. What can I get everyone to drink? Your father is drinking scotch, and I'm having a glass of white wine."

Which meant that Marly would be expected to have white wine as well, and Sam could either have scotch or wine, but it was always implied that a real man would go for the scotch.

"How about a martini?" he said.

There was nothing but silence. Marly shot her father a glance. Every muscle in his face had gone rigid. He knew Sam was goading him, but he wouldn't rise to the bait until he was certain he had the upper hand.

Marly shifted her attention to her mother, who was already fussing with the sleeves of her dress. "I'm not sure we have vermouth," she murmured.

Sam held up the paper bag he'd carried in with him. "I stopped by the liquor store on my way over. Allow me to do the honors." He strode to the bar and began to mix and shake up a storm.

When he finished, he carried over a tray with three glasses. "Mother?"

She perched on the edge of the sofa, knees pressed together, posture as perfect as always. "Oh,

I don't know.'' She glanced at her husband. ''It's been years since I've had anything stronger than wine.''

''It won't kill you,'' Sam assured her. ''You might even enjoy it.'' When she continued to hesitate, he urged softly, ''Come on, Mom. Live a little.''

She gave a nervous laugh and accepted one of the glasses.

''Marly?''

''Don't mind if I do.'' Marly didn't usually drink anything stronger than wine, either, but not because of her father's disapproval. She'd had a few bad experiences with alcohol in college.

Sam took the last drink and clinked glasses with Marly. ''Here's to your health. Not a bad toast, considering everything that's going on around here.''

Marly grimaced. ''Don't remind me.''

''Oh,'' her mother said, nursing her drink. ''I heard about Ricky Morales on the radio. How awful for his family.''

''I wouldn't waste my sympathy on the likes of him.'' Wesley Jessop reached for the bottle of scotch he kept nearby. ''The damn fool shot himself. I've got no sympathy for cowards.''

''I still feel sorry for his family,'' Andrea murmured. ''I should probably give his mother a call.''

Marly glanced up in surprise. ''You know his mother?''

''Not well. She goes to my church.''

''Your mother has a new church, did she tell you?'' There was something in her father's tone, in his eyes that made Marly shiver again. Something was going on here tonight. The tension was even thicker than usual.

"I'm sure the children aren't interested in my church activities," Andrea said nervously.

The housekeeper announced dinner then, and they filed into the dining room, her father taking his place at the head of the table, her mother at the other end, and Sam and Marly facing one another. Catching her gaze, he gave her a conspiratorial wink that immediately lifted her spirits.

And just as quickly, her father dashed them by grumbling about the salad dressing, then the overcooked vegetables and the undercooked pot roast. Or perhaps it was the other way around. Everything tasted fine to Marly, and as she ate, she tried her best to tune out her father's insults, which were directed at her mother even though Andrea hadn't personally prepared the meal.

"So, Mom, what's this about your joining a new church?" she asked curiously.

Her mother's fork clattered against her plate. She quickly straightened it as she muttered an apology.

Her father laid aside his knife and fork as well. "Yes, Andrea. Why don't you tell the children about your new church?"

"I don't think they'd be interested—"

"Oh, I think they would. Especially Marlene." Her father's frigid gaze moved from his wife to his daughter. "Seems your mother has taken up with your old boyfriend."

Someone gasped. Marly thought it might have been her.

Her father nodded. "It's true. Your mother has become infatuated with your discarded fiancé."

Marly felt the blood drain from her face as she stared at her mother's frozen expression. "What's he talking about?" she asked softly.

Her gaze met Marly's briefly before dropping to her plate. "I've been attending services at the Glorious Way Church."

"Since when?" Marly asked in astonishment.

"A few months." Her mother stared furiously at her plate. "I enjoy Joshua's sermons. I find them very inspiring. That's all there is to it."

"I'd say there's a little more to it than that," her husband goaded. "Your mother is working at the church now, Marlene. I believe she has your old job. Isn't that right, Andrea?"

"I've been helping out ever since Mrs. Abbott died. I volunteer a few hours a week—"

"That's a new one, isn't it?" Wesley cut in. "A mother following in her daughter's footsteps? First her church, then her boyfriend and now her job."

Andrea put a hand to her mouth, but when she glanced up, her eyes were gleaming with something Marly had never seen there before. She wasn't sure if it was defiance...or guilt.

Marly's stomach churned, and she knew she wouldn't be able to force down another bite.

Best diet in the world, she thought dryly. Dinner with the folks.

But apparently her father's appetite wasn't diminished. He picked up his knife and fork and calmly resumed eating. "What's next, I wonder? Rush's bed?"

Her mother made a tiny sound of protest, and Sam said through clenched teeth, "Shut up."

Wesley stopped eating. "What did you say?"

Sam glared at him. "You heard me. I said shut the hell up. If Mother's found someone else, more power to her. It's about damn time."

Her father's face turned scarlet with rage. "How dare you speak to me that way? I won't stand for it, do you hear me? I won't brook that kind of insolence in my own home. I've a good mind to—"

"What?" Sam's smile was chilling. "Take me down a peg or two?"

"Don't tempt me," Wesley warned.

"Come on." Sam shoved back his chair. "I've been waiting for this my whole life."

"You think you're man enough to take me on?" Wesley sneered. "You think I don't know about you? You left the army because you couldn't cut it. You're nothing but a—" He broke off, his face contorting in what Marly first thought was fury. He turned a darker shade of red and made a rasping sound in the back of his throat as he lifted his hands to his neck.

"My God," Marly said in horror. "He's choking."

Everything seemed to happen in fast motion then. As Marly sprang up from the table and rushed toward her father, she caught a glimpse of her brother's face. Sam remained seated, his gaze fixed on their father, and for one brief moment, Marly could have sworn he was still smiling.

## Chapter Eleven

Marly waited in the upstairs hall for her mother to come out of the master bedroom. When she finally did, she took Marly's arm and they walked down the stairs together.

"How is he?" Marly asked.

"He's resting. The paramedics said he'll be fine."

"They also said he needed to go to the hospital and get checked out," Marly reminded her.

They were at the bottom of the stairs now, and her mother turned to face her. "You know your father."

*Yes, and I thought I knew you.* Marly gazed into her mother's eyes. Tonight the woman who'd given birth to her suddenly seemed like a stranger. Marly wanted to ask her about her father's accusations. Wanted to warn her away from Joshua Rush—not because she still harbored feelings for him herself. Not because of jealousy or resentment, but because he was a man exactly like her father.

As if sensing her confusion, her mother gave her a tender smile. "You saved his life."

"I didn't do it alone. Sam had a hand in it, too."
After that split second of hesitation, Sam had been
by her side in an instant, helping her to lay their
father on the floor once she'd dislodged the block-
age from his throat, counting off the beats while she
performed CPR. But then, when the paramedics arrived, he'd simply disappeared.

"Yes, but you were the first one to his side. You
were the one who got him breathing again," her
mother said softly. "Before tonight, I had a hard
time picturing you as a police officer. But not anymore. Now I know how capable you truly are." Her
mother's eyes gleamed with quiet pride as she lifted
a hand and placed it gently on Marly's cheek. "You
really are an extraordinary woman. My daughter, the
cop."

It was one of the most touching moments Marly
could ever remember sharing with her mother. She
didn't want to let it go. Her eyes misted with tears.
"Thank you, Mama."

She turned her head slightly, grazing her mother's
hand with a kiss, feeling the calloused ridge of the
scar that slashed across her mother's wrist.

A scar that no one ever talked about. A scar that
her mother always kept hidden beneath long sleeves.

A scar that matched the one on her other wrist.

SAM STOOD ON THE PORCH watching the rain when
Marly came outside. "I thought you'd left," she
said in surprise.

"Just needed some air. How is he?"

"He'll be fine. He won't go to the hospital, though."

"Yeah, I know. I spoke to the paramedics before they left."

Marly came up and stood beside him at the rail. "It seems like it's been raining forever," she said with a sigh.

"You used to like the rain," Sam reminded her. "You always said that when it rained you didn't have to feel guilty for staying inside, curled up with a book."

Marly gave a fake shudder. "I was such a geek."

"We were both strange kids," Sam said. "But is it any wonder? Look how we were raised."

Marly put out her hand and caught raindrops in her palm. "Do you hate him, Sam?"

"Don't you?"

"Sometimes I do." She closed her fist around the raindrops. "Sometimes I just wonder why he is the way he is. He didn't have the greatest mother—"

"Stop making excuses for him," Sam said angrily.

"I'm not," Marly defended.

"Yes, you are, but it's a waste of time." Sam turned back to the rain. "He is what he is. Just accept it and move on. You'll be a lot happier."

"Are you happy, Sam?"

He hesitated. "I'm content, I guess. I accept the old man for who and what he is, and I've done the same for myself."

And just who are you? Marly wondered. She thought about that scene in his kitchen, the way Max

Perry had placed his hand on Sam's arm, and she suddenly wanted to ask what it meant.

But how did you ask your brother, a grown man, a man whom she'd lost touch with for years when he'd been in the service, a man who had come back home wary and secretive, something so personal?

Besides, if there was something he wanted her to know, he would tell her, wouldn't he?

But what if he was waiting for her to ask? What if he had been waiting years for her to ask?

Marly glanced up, meeting his gaze and seeing in those dark depths a deep and infinite loneliness that she had never fully understood.

He was her brother, and she loved him dearly, trusted him with her very life, but Marly suddenly realized that she had never really known him.

WHEN SHE GOT BACK TO HER apartment that night, Deacon waited under the covered landing just outside her door. Marly halted when she spotted him, their previous conversation rushing back to her. *"I was trained to kill. And I did so with ruthless precision."*

She wasn't at all sure she wanted to resume that conversation. Or, more to the point, she wasn't at all sure she wanted to be alone with a man who was either utterly demented or a ruthless killer. Or both.

But she found herself walking toward him just the same. When she stood next to him under the cover, she glanced up reluctantly, almost afraid to make eye contact. "What are you doing here?"

He shoved his hands into his jacket pockets. "I had to see you."

"How did you find out where I live?"

"It's a small town, Marly. It wasn't difficult."

He turned then, and she gasped when she saw his face. "Oh, my God," she whispered. "What happened to you?" Before she could stop herself, she put up a hand to tentatively touch one of the bruises.

Deacon winced but didn't pull back. "I fell down some stairs," he muttered.

"Why do I have a feeling you aren't joking about that?" Marly said. "Are you okay?"

He shrugged. "I'll live."

"Maybe you should go to the hospital and get checked out."

"I'm fine. But we need to talk, Marly." His hands came out of his pockets then, and he was suddenly looming over her, his eyes gleaming in the dark as he gazed down at her.

"What about?" she asked nervously.

"I told you that first day that the man we're looking for is someone between the ages of thirty and forty, with a military background he doesn't like to talk about. Remember?"

She nodded.

"I also asked if you knew anyone who fit that description." His gaze on her deepened, intensified, until Marly knew she couldn't look away if she tried. "I'm asking you again."

Her stomach quivered with nerves. "What are you getting at?"

"I want you to tell me about your brother."

"Sam? What about him?"

"When he was in the service, did he stay in touch with the family? Or were there long periods of time when you didn't hear from him? When you didn't know where he was?"

Marly didn't like where this conversation was going. "That's none of your business," she said angrily.

"Just answer the question. Or are you afraid to answer it?"

Marly glared up at him. "Don't try to manipulate me. You think I don't recognize what you're doing? I lived with the master of those tactics for years." Her voice was edged with scorn. "But I'll answer your question anyway. No, Sam didn't keep in touch. We didn't hear from him for months at a time. Almost a year once. There were times when I didn't know if he was alive or dead. But that doesn't prove anything. My brother isn't a killer," she said through clenched teeth.

"He fits the profile."

"So do a lot of other people in this town." Marly still couldn't look away from that grim gaze.

"When he came home, were there gaps in his memories? Things he should have remembered but didn't?"

Marly didn't want to answer any more of his questions. He was hitting too many nerves. Sam *had* been different when he'd gotten out of the service. He'd been moody, secretive, nothing more than a polite stranger at times. And he hadn't been able to remember things from their childhood, little things that shouldn't have mattered but somehow did. At least to her.

"When you were kids, was Sam ever sent away?" Deacon persisted.

*Don't answer that,* a little voice warned her, but she heard herself saying, "When he was ten, he was sent away to a military academy. He was gone for two years, and when he came back…"

"He was different that time, too, wasn't he?"

Marly put a hand to her mouth. "How do you know all this?"

"Because there are others out there just like him. Some were taken with the cooperation of their parents, others by force. Most of them were males between the ages of nine and twelve who exhibited superior athletic and academic skills, as well as a certain amount of psychic ability. Others, like me, were recruited from the ranks of the regular military, mostly from Special Forces. We willingly underwent the experiments because we thought we were serving our country and all of humanity. But we were wrong. The Montauk Project wasn't about the betterment of mankind. It was about power."

Marly balled her hands into fists. "I don't understand half of what you're saying, but I do know this. My brother isn't a killer."

"What if I told you he may have been the one who attacked me tonight?"

Marly gasped. "You said you fell down some stairs."

"After being bashed in the back of the head."

Her heart quickened. "Where were you?"

"In your brother's house."

"In my—" Marly's gaze shot back to his. "Sam was with me tonight. He couldn't have been the one who attacked you. And by the way, just what the hell were you doing in his house?"

"He was with you all evening?"

Marly's mind flashed back to earlier in the evening. Sam had been late getting to her parents' house. He said he'd stopped at a liquor store. "We had dinner together," she said. "And it was something of a traumatic event, so if you'll excuse me—"

Deacon caught her arm. "Don't overlook the obvious, Marly."

"What's that supposed to mean?"

"It means you have to keep an open mind. You can't rule out any suspect at this point."

"Suspect?" Her tone turned frigid. "I'm not even convinced that a crime has been committed, except for you breaking into my brother's house. I could take you in for that, you know. Throw the book at you."

Somehow she'd backed up against the door of her apartment, and Deacon was standing over her, his body planted in front of her so that she couldn't escape. For the first time that night, Marly felt real terror, but not for her own safety.

"You take me in, nobody's going to be looking for the killer."

"How do I know you're not making all this up?" she challenged. "How do I know *you're* not the killer?"

His smile was humorless. "At least you're admitting now that there is one. That's progress."

"I never admitted anything."

One brow lifted slightly. "You still need proof?"

She licked her lips. "You can't prove the impossible. You can't reach inside my head and control my thoughts."

"Are you that certain?" He reached up and ran the back of his hand along her jawline.

"Don't touch me."

He dropped his hand to his side. "You're free to turn and go inside your apartment anytime you want to. I'm not stopping you."

But he was. Maybe not with his mind, but with his presence. With the attraction that sizzled between them even as Marly tried to deny it.

"You've done something to me. I don't know what it is, but—"

He wove his hands through her hair, bending to nuzzle her neck. "You want me," he whispered against her ear.

God help her, she did. It was like a physical ache.

He was kissing her then, long deep kisses that made Marly quiver from head to toe, that made her heart feel as if it were about to explode inside her chest. He was touching her, too. His hands were all over her. Sliding her jacket down her arms. Slipping his hands up her skirt. Exploring her so intimately, Marly could barely breathe. She could feel something building inside her. Something powerful. Something she couldn't control.

She leaned against the door, eyes closed, trembling and terrified.

"I want you, too," he murmured in her ear. "I want to pick you up and carry you inside your apartment, lay you on the bed and undress you slowly. I want to touch you all over, taste every inch of you, and then I want to be inside you—"

Marly shuddered against his hand, and then turned her head away, humiliated and humbled. "Oh, God."

"Marly—"

He said her name so tenderly, tears spurted behind her eyes. "Maybe you do control my thoughts," she whispered. "Maybe you do have some kind of power over me. Because I don't lose control like that. That wasn't me."

"Yes, it was. This is the real you. You're a strong, passionate woman. The sooner you accept that reality, the better off you'll be."

She still wouldn't look at him. "Why don't you just go to hell?" she said without much conviction.

"I've already been there, Marly."

He turned then and headed out into the rain. She watched him walk across the parking lot to his truck, get inside, and drive off. She watched even when his taillights had faded into the night.

She watched the darkness, knowing that she hadn't seen the last of Deacon Cage.

MARLY AWAKENED WITH A START, certain that someone was in her apartment. She could sense him.

He was out there somewhere, rummaging through her personal things, violating her private space.

Her heart pounding with fear, she reached over and retrieved her gun from the nightstand drawer. Easing up in bed, she clutched the cold metal in both hands as she peered through the darkness.

He was still there. She couldn't see him. Couldn't hear him. But she could feel him.

What should she do? Marly wondered frantically. Her first instinct was to cower under the covers and hope that he would go away. But cops didn't cower. Cops took control of the situation.

Still gripping her weapon, Marly shoved back the quilt and swung her legs over the side of the bed. Then she froze in terror because suddenly she knew. The killer had come to give her a warning.

But he wasn't inside her apartment. He was inside her head.

# *Chapter Twelve*

Navarro called Marly into his office for a meeting
the following morning. In addition to Joshua Rush
and Max Perry, there were four newcomers present,
all pastors of local churches who were eager to join
the community outreach program that Max had
agreed to spearhead.

Marly sat off to the side, pretending to take notes,
but her mind kept straying back to the previous evening. The moment she'd seen Joshua in Navarro's
office, she'd thought about her father's accusations,
and she couldn't help wondering about Joshua's relationship with her mother.

Was there really something going on between
them?

Reluctantly Marly glanced up, her gaze sweeping
over him. He was dressed in khaki chinos and a light
blue sweater that matched his eyes perfectly. His
hair was combed in a boyish style, and his features
were arranged into lines of concern as he listened to
Navarro.

But those eyes gave him away every time, Marly

thought. At least for her they did. They were cold, cynical and mocking.

The idea of Joshua and her mother...*together* made Marly physically ill. She had a difficult time believing that her mother, after living under her husband's tyranny for years, would fall for another man just like him.

But then, people often repeated their mistakes. Life could be a vicious circle, and her mother was vulnerable and naïve. And Marly knew better than anyone how charming and persuasive Joshua could be when he set his mind to something. What better way to get back at her for breaking up with him than by seducing her mother?

Although maybe she was flattering herself, Marly conceded. Maybe this didn't have anything to do with her. Her mother was still a beautiful, desirable woman. It wasn't inconceivable that Joshua simply saw her, wanted her, and, in spite of their age difference, went after her like he had with all his other conquests.

Marly couldn't believe she'd once been so gullible and stupid. Looking back, it was easy to see how the attention and gifts he'd showered on her were all part of the seduction. How his outward charm and charisma had blinded her to the subtle cruelty, to the creeping oppression.

Thank God she'd discovered what he was really like before it was too late. Before she married him. Before she ended up like her mother.

Could he be the one? Marly thought with a sudden shiver. A cold-blooded killer?

Last night, alone and frightened in her bedroom, she'd almost convinced herself that Deacon was on to something. In light of what had happened between them earlier, maybe she'd even wanted to believe him. Wanted to believe that her reckless behavior was caused by something other than her attraction to a man she barely knew.

What if it was true? What if someone in this town, perhaps in this very room, had the kind of military background and extraordinary skills that Deacon had warned her about?

Marly's gaze lit on Tony Navarro, and she remembered all the talk that had circulated around town when he'd first arrived, including the rumor that he was an ex-Navy SEAL. He'd never confirmed or denied any of the buzz. He didn't talk about his personal life at all. Marly didn't even know where he was from. He'd come to town one day, been hired on the spot by the town council, and now she had to wonder what had convinced them so quickly? His qualifications? His personality? Or…something else? Had he used extraordinary measures to convince them?

Marly would have laughed at her own speculation except for one not so amusing fact. Four people were dead. Four people in Mission Creek had taken their own lives over a ten-day period. Four people who had given no indication to their friends and loved ones that they were depressed, let alone suicidal.

Gracie Abbott, David Shelley, Amber Tyson and Ricky Morales.

Four people who, with the exception of David and Amber, were linked to one another only through a loose connection to the school.

And to the Glorious Way Church.

A dark premonition slipped over Marly as her thoughts once again turned to Joshua. Strangely enough, she knew very little about his background. He'd told her the basics. He'd grown up in the South, had attended seminary school in Memphis, and had been offered the job at the nondenominational church on Sixth Street after his predecessor had accepted a position in El Paso.

He was an only child, and his parents had died years ago, when he was still in school. He had no family to speak of which was why he'd been anxious to accept the position in Mission Creek. The community was close-knit and supportive. In other words, a substitute family for him.

Since he'd become pastor, the congregation at the Glorious Way had more than tripled. He'd even attracted worshipers from the surroundings communities, and they'd become more than just his faithful congregation. They were his followers. His devotees. Their adoration was such that Joshua had become almost a religion unto himself.

Her gaze moved to Max Perry, and she realized that she didn't know much about him, either. He'd assumed the position of guidance counselor at the high school when the former counselor had died tragically in an automobile accident over the Christmas holidays. Max's timely availability had seemed like a stroke of luck for the school, but what if it had been something other than luck?

He turned suddenly, catching Marly's gaze, and she glanced away.

She was starting to suspect every man in Mission Creek, especially the ones she knew little about. The ones between the ages of thirty and forty. The ones who perhaps had a military background.

Deacon Cage had planted that suspicion in her head when, in fact, he was the one she knew the least about. He was the one who best fit his own profile.

"Marly?"

She started at the sound of her name. When she glanced up, Navarro lifted a brow. "Any questions?"

Marly glanced down at her notebook. The page was blank. "No sir."

"In that case, I'd say it's time we all get to work."

Marly rose and walked quickly out of the room before anyone had a chance to stop her.

"DO ME A FAVOR," Marly said a few minutes later as she pulled on her jacket.

Patty Fuentes perched on the corner of her desk. "What's that?" The moment Marly had come out of Navarro's office, Patty had ambled over, hoping for a nice long chat. But Marly had no time for gossip today even though she always enjoyed Patty's company. The receptionist—one of only a handful of civilians who worked for the police department—was gregarious and outrageous in ways Marly could never hope to be.

"If anyone asks where I've gone, tell them I'm out on patrol."

Patty examined her beautifully manicured nails. "Sure, no problem. And if someone needs to reach you?"

"Cover for me. Just give me an hour."

One glamorous brow arched as Patty glanced up. "Now you've got me dying of curiosity. What are you up to, girlfriend?"

"I just need to run an errand."

Patty's gaze narrowed. "Nuh-uh, you're up to something. You've got guilt written all over your face." She cocked her head, giving Marly a long scrutiny. "If I didn't know better..."

"If you didn't know better, what?" Marly said absently.

Patty leaned forward, lowering her voice. "If I didn't know better, I'd say you have the look of a woman who had one helluva good time in bed last night."

Marly blushed furiously. "Anyone ever tell you that you have a dirty mind?"

"Yes, and your point is?" Patty folded her arms, still watching her. "Who is he?" she demanded. "Come on, give. I want details."

"You're crazy," Marly muttered. But it was difficult because the images she'd tried to keep at bay all morning suddenly blossomed inside her head.

*"I want you, too. I want to pick you up and carry you inside your apartment, lay you on the bed, and undress you slowly. I want to touch you all over,*

*taste every inch of you, and then I want to be inside you—''*

Marly's heart started to race, just thinking about Deacon Cage, remembering the feel of his mouth and hands, wondering, in spite of herself, what it would be like to have him inside her.

*God in heaven, what is* wrong *with you?*

"Look at you. You're as red as a beet," Patty teased. "And you're not going to tell me who he is, are you?"

Marly ducked her head, pretending to gather up papers from her desk. "There's nothing to tell."

"You know what I think?" Patty gave her a knowing smile. "I think that twinkle in your eyes and that blush on your face has something to do with that guy who came in here the other day."

"What guy?"

"The one who looked like he could go from zero to bad ass in about two seconds flat. Deacon Cage, I think his name was."

Marly pushed back her chair and stood. "Your imagination is working overtime."

Patty grinned. "Maybe. Wouldn't be the first time. But I do know this. Joshua Rush never put a glow on your face like that—"

She stopped short, muttered something under her breath, and Marly glanced up. Joshua stood not five feet from her desk, and judging by the angry glint in his eyes, he'd overheard every word of their conversation.

MARVIN BOLT, AMBER TYSON'S stepfather, answered the door so quickly, Marly wondered if he'd been watching for her out the window.

"Thanks for agreeing to see me," she said as she stepped into the tiled foyer.

Marvin closed the door behind her and turned with a scowl. "Ruby's gone out to run some errands. She'll be back in a couple of hours so you'll have to make this quick. I don't want her to come home and find you here. She's been through enough."

Marly nodded. "I understand. This won't take long."

Marvin rubbed his chin in puzzlement. "I still don't understand why you want to see Amber's room."

"I'm just trying to understand what happened to her," Marly explained, although she knew the excuse sounded lame. "Maybe it'll help us prevent it from happening to someone else."

"I hope you're right." He led the way upstairs and down the hall to Amber's bedroom, pausing at the threshold as if he didn't have the heart to walk inside. "This is her room. I don't know where Ruby put all that stuff Navarro brought over, but I imagine it's in here somewhere."

Marly glanced at him in surprise. "Navarro returned Amber's personal effects?"

"He brought a box by here the other night. I thought that was real nice of him though I can't say he's an overly friendly fellow. But we appreciated the gesture."

A gesture that seemed totally out of character for

Navarro, Marly thought. Normally he would have
sent one of his deputies on such a mission. But she
supposed that just proved how little she really knew
about him.

Amber's bedroom was a typical teenage girl's
space, cluttered and overly decorated in shades of
blue with a faux fur throw on the bed and posters
of her favorite bands tacked to the walls. Marly
glanced at Marvin, reluctant to invade his step-
daughter's space. "All right if I have a look
around?"

"That's what you're here for, isn't it?"

Marly stepped inside and slowly walked around
the room, stopping to examine a bulletin board that
held some of Amber's personal mementos. Photo-
graphs of classmates, ribbons from a homecoming
corsage, a science award signed by Sam.

Marly stared at the award, momentarily taken
aback by seeing her brother's name in the dead girl's
bedroom.

"Amber was real proud of that award," Marvin
said from the doorway. He shoved his hands into
the pocket of his faded jeans. "She was a good stu-
dent. A good girl. Went to church every Sunday,
although I can't say I approved of the one she attended."

Marly glanced over her shoulder. "She attended
the Glorious Way, didn't she?"

He nodded, his expression grim.

"Why didn't you approve?" Marly asked.

"Because that preacher they got over there,

Brother Rush, they call him, he's one slick opera-
tor,'' Marvin said scornfully. "He reminds me of
one of those tele-evangelists. They preach one thing
on Sunday so they can beg for your money, then
they go out and do whatever the hell they want
every other day of the week.''

He had Joshua pegged all right, Marly thought
dryly.

Marvin's features hardened. ''I didn't like her being so chummy with that guy, and I told Ruby so.
It wasn't right, him being a grown man and Amber
still a kid, just barely eighteen. But Ruby wouldn't
hear anything against him.''

''What do you mean by chummy?'' Marly tried
to ask casually.

''He'd call here after school and ask Amber to
come down to the church for first one reason and
then another. She was a whiz with computers, and
he always claimed he needed her help. Then he'd
drive her home, sometimes after dark. I didn't like
it, but it didn't do me much good to say so, me being
just her stepfather and all.''

''Did you and Amber have problems?''

''No more than normal, I guess. It's hard accepting someone new into the family. I understood that.
Ruby and I just got married a few months ago, but
it seemed to me things were going along fine until
Amber started going to that church. Then she
changed.''

''Changed how?''

He shrugged. ''She was always real easygoing before, but after that, she became moody and secretive, like she was keeping things from us."

"You don't have any idea what it might have been?"

He glanced away. "I might have had my suspicions. But I kept them to myself. Maybe I shouldn't have. Maybe I should have tried to talk to her. Find out what was going on. Maybe then she wouldn't have done what she did, but...I guess we'll never know now, will we?"

He turned then, shoulders hunched, and disappeared down the hallway. Marly could hear his footsteps on the stairs and a moment later, the muffled sound of the TV.

Alone, she walked over to the dresser and gazed down at the jumble of lipsticks, eye shadows and perfumes, marveling at such an expensive assortment for a teenage girl. No drugstore cosmetics in the lot. Marly tended to notice such things because she hadn't been allowed to wear makeup as a teen. She hadn't owned so much as a lip gloss until she'd gone away to college.

Funny how that still rankled. And strange that now that she could wear makeup whenever she wanted, she frequently chose not to.

A tiny gold cross hung from the corner of Amber's mirror, and Marly picked it up, feeling the cool metal in her palm.

Could Joshua be the link that connected all the suicides? she wondered. David and Amber had both been active in the youth group, and according to Marvin, Amber may have had an even closer relationship with Joshua. Gracie Abbot had taught Sunday school class and worked in the office, and while Ricky Morales hadn't been a member of the church, his mother was.

And then there was Nona's assertion that something had been going on between Ricky and Crystal Bishop. What if Crystal had taken back up with Joshua, and Ricky had somehow found out—

*Wait a minute,* Marly warned herself. *You're starting to sound as if you think the victims really were murdered. You're starting to sound as if you believe Deacon Cage.*

And if she believed him about the killer, didn't she have to believe him about…the other? That he had the ability to control another person's thoughts. That he could manipulate someone's mind into making them do whatever he wanted.

How else could she explain her behavior with him?

If he could arouse that kind of response in her by just kissing her and touching her…

She wouldn't think about that now, Marly decided. She needed to concentrate on the business at hand, and Deacon Cage had become too much of a distraction. Too much of a threat to her peace of mind.

Walking over to the nightstand, she picked up a book to see what Amber had been reading. It was a copy of *The Scarlet Letter.* An assignment for English class, no doubt. The symbolism of an illicit and an inappropriate relationship was probably nothing more than a coincidence.

But as Marly leafed through the book, a photo-
graph fell out and she bent to pick it up. Then froze.

It was a snapshot of her brother. Of Sam and several of his students, to be precise. They looked to
be huddled over a science project, and Marly recognized both Amber and David Shelley in the group.
They were standing side by side, but Amber's gaze
was on Sam and there was something about the way
she was smiling at him...about the look in her eyes
that seemed...intimate.

Someone else had been caught in the frame.
Marly lifted the picture to the light, trying to make
out the shadowy figure in the background. She
couldn't be sure, but she thought it might be Max
Perry.

"Marly?"

Deacon's voice startled her so badly, she almost
dropped the book. Marly turned to find him staring
at her from the doorway.

Quickly she replaced the snapshot in the book and
closed it. "What are you doing here?"

His gaze seemed to darken as he watched her. As
if he knew she was hiding something from him. "I
saw you leave the station."

"And you followed me?" Her tone grew indignant, but as much out of guilt as genuine outrage.

"I thought you could use my help." Slowly, he
walked into the room and glanced around.

"With what?"

"Your investigation." His tone seemed to challenge her. "You're here looking for clues, aren't
you? Some evidence that will point you to the

killer?'' His gaze dropped to the book she still held in her hand, and Marly wondered suddenly if he could do more than just control thoughts. Could he also read minds?

''I'm looking for the truth,'' she said, placing the book back on the nightstand.

''The truth?''

''About David and Amber. I think we may have jumped to conclusions regarding their suicides,'' she admitted. Reluctantly she told him about her visit from Amber's cousin. ''If we were wrong about the motivation in that case, if it was something other than a teenage suicide pact, then I can't help wondering what else we might have gotten wrong. Maybe we missed some clues that could help us figure out what's going on around here.''

''And you think this older man Amber was interested in might have something to do with her death?''

Marly hesitated. ''I don't know. But something Lisa told me has been bothering me. She went to Navarro with the same information she gave me, and he told her to just forget about it. It wouldn't make any difference. The case was closed, and talk about Amber and an older man would only hurt Amber's family.''

Deacon was still walking slowly around the room. ''Sounds logical.''

''Not if you know Navarro. He's a meticulous investigator. I can't imagine him sweeping any kind of information or evidence under a rug just to spare someone's feelings. I can't help thinking...''

When she didn't finish her thought, Deacon turned. "What?"

Marly pushed her hair behind her ears. "I guess I can't help wondering if he could have been the older man Amber was infatuated with. If that's the reason he wanted to keep Lisa Potter silent."

Something glinted in Deacon's eyes. "You think it's possible Amber was involved with Navarro?"

Marly shrugged. "It's not inconceivable. Every female over the age of twelve has had a crush on Navarro since he came to town."

"Including you?" Deacon had his back to her now. Marly couldn't see his expression, but there was something in his voice...

If she didn't know better, she'd swear he was jealous.

But that didn't make sense. There was nothing between them. They were still virtually strangers.

And yet from the moment she'd first met Deacon, Marly hadn't been able to get him out of her head. Even after the insane things he'd told her about mind control and psychokinesis, even after he'd practically accused her brother of being a killer, she still hadn't been able to resist his kiss last night.

He was standing in front of the dresser, and their gazes met in the mirror. His stare raked over her body, reminding her all too vividly that in one very intimate way, they were no longer strangers.

"What's this?" he murmured, reaching up to pluck something off the mirror.

Marly walked over to join him. He held a tiny

paper eye in his palm, one with rays of light emanating from the iris.

"That's a symbol used by the Glorious Way Church," Marly said. "Joshua's church."

Deacon glanced up. "She had it taped to the mirror. What do you suppose that means?"

"Maybe it was a reminder that a higher power constantly watched over her." Or that Joshua did. Marly shivered. "Her stepfather seems to think that there may have been something going on between Amber and Joshua."

Deacon pressed the eye to the mirror with his thumb. "What do you think about that?"

"I think anything is possible where Joshua Rush is concerned."

"Even murder?"

Marly glanced away. "I don't know. I know I don't trust him."

Her answer seemed to satisfy Deacon for the moment. He moved across the room and studied the same bulletin board she'd examined earlier. And she knew he would see exactly what she'd seen.

After a moment, he turned. "Sam was Amber's teacher, wasn't he?"

"So?" Marly knew exactly where the conversation was leading. She hadn't liked his accusations last night, and she liked them even less this morning. She wanted to tell him again that her brother wasn't a killer. She wanted to scream it at the top of her lungs. Instead she folded her arms and watched him.

He came back over to where she stood next to the bed. "You say you want to find the truth?"

Reaching around her, he picked up the copy of *The Scarlet Letter* from the nightstand and placed it in her hands. "Then don't ignore the clues, Marly. Start listening to your instincts. No matter what they tell you."

DORIS KEATING PEERED anxiously out her window before drawing back her door. She was a tiny woman, less than five feet tall and weighing no more than ninety pounds, Marly was certain. She'd known the woman for years. Marly's parents lived just down the street, and when Marly was younger, Mrs. Keating had been her piano teacher.

"Come in, Marly." The older woman stood back for her to enter. "My goodness, you got here fast. I didn't expect you until much later."

Marly carefully wiped her damp feet on the welcome mat before she stepped inside Mrs. Keating's fastidious home. "I happened to be in the area so I decided to come on by."

"Are you on your way to see your mother?" the woman inquired politely.

"No, ma'am. I'm still on duty."

"Oh, dear." Mrs. Keating's gaze took in Marly's uniform. "There hasn't been another death, has there?"

"No, it's nothing like that," Marly said gently. "Like I told you on the phone, I need to take a look inside Miss Gracie's house. It's purely routine. I just need to check out something for our files, and I figured since you lived next door to her for so long, you probably had a key to each other's houses."

"Well, you're right about that. I do have a key to Gracie's house. She and I weren't just neighbors, you know. We were dear, dear friends." While she rambled on, she crossed the room and fished a key out of one of the ceramic shoes she kept grouped together in a walnut curio cabinet. She brought the key back over to Marly.

"Now as soon as you're finished, you bring that right back to me, hear? I know Gracie's never going to need it again, but she gave it to me for safekeeping. I wouldn't feel right letting just any Tom, Dick or Harry traipse through her home."

"I understand. I'll bring it back." Marly started for the door, then turned. "Have you seen anyone coming in or out of Miss Gracie's house in the last few days?"

"No. Well, just that nice young man from the school."

Marly's heart skipped a beat. "What nice young man?"

"The scholarly looking gentleman. Mr. Perry."

Marly came back into the room. "Max Perry?"

Mrs. Keating nodded. "He's interested in buying Gracie's house, and he wondered if I knew who he should contact about it. I told him that as far as I knew Gracie's niece in San Antonio would oversee the sale. I gave him her number and he seemed very appreciative. We had a most enjoyable visit. He's quite the conversationalist and so beautifully mannered. Oh, and such gorgeous hands." She sighed. "I certainly wouldn't mind having him for a neighbor."

"Did Mr. Perry ask to borrow your key?" Marly asked.

"Oh, no. That was my idea. I didn't think it would do any harm for him to have a quick look around." She bit her lip. "I didn't do anything wrong, did I?"

"No, of course not." Marly gave her a reassuring smile. "I'll bring the key back when I'm finished."

"See that you do, dear."

The door closed behind her, and Marly crossed the yard in the cold drizzle to Gracie Abbott's house. Letting herself in through the front door, she took a moment to acquaint herself with the layout, then hurried down the hallway to the kitchen. A door in the laundry room connected to the garage, and as Marly stepped inside, she automatically reached for the light switch. When the light didn't come on, she wondered if the electricity had already been disconnected.

Two small windows looked out on the backyard, but the overcast day didn't provide much illumination. Marly got out her flashlight and switched it on.

The garage was spacious enough to accommodate Miss Gracie's ten-year-old sedan, as well as her gardening tools and the usual accumulation of odds and ends. Picking her way across the concrete floor, Marly approached the car with a growing sense of unease. She found it more than a little creepy being in the same room where someone had died so recently. That was an aspect of her job she didn't think she'd ever get used to.

Opening the car door on the driver's side, she

angled the flashlight beam around the interior. Leaning inside, she checked the radio dial. It was set to KBRT, the local station. If Miss Gracie had had her radio turned on when she drove home from church the day she died, she would have been listening to "Gloomy Sunday" as she pulled into the garage.

Was it possible she'd called in and requested the song herself? Did she know about the legend associated with "Gloomy Sunday?" Had she planned even that small detail of her suicide?

Or was there something more subtle at work here? Something more sinister? Was a killer using that song to send Marly a message?

*"You say you want to find the truth? Then don't ignore the clues, Marly. Start listening to your instincts. No matter what they tell you."*

But Marly didn't want to listen to her instincts. She didn't want to dwell on the possibility that the song really was a clue because it could only mean one thing. It had been left by someone close to her.

Her heart pounding, she backed out of the car and as she straightened, she caught a glimpse of something at the window. A shadow was there one moment and gone so quickly the next that Marly wondered if her overwrought imagination had conjured it. Like seeing her grandmother's ghost in her bedroom window after waking from a nightmare.

And it was almost just as spooky, Marly decided, as she hurried across the garage and let herself back into Miss Gracie's house. She retraced her route through the kitchen and was halfway down the hallway when she heard a tiny noise, like the creak of a stair beneath someone's foot.

Marly halted in her tracks, listening for another telltale sound. But she heard nothing. Not even a ticking clock or a passing car. There was nothing but silence. The same unnatural quiet she'd noticed at Ricky Morales house the day she'd found his body.

The hair on the back of her neck rose as she remained frozen in place. There was still no sound, nothing to give away an intruder, but she knew she wasn't alone. She could sense another presence, just as she had the night before in her apartment. But this time, the intruder was physically there, hiding somewhere in Gracie Abbott's house.

As quietly as she could, Marly drew her weapon. Sliding off the safety, she clutched the gun in both hands as she eased down the hall toward the foyer.

The front door was ajar, as if to make her think he'd gone back out, but Marly knew that wasn't the case. He was still there. Still waiting.

And then she felt him.

Inside her mind.

It was a sensation like nothing she'd ever experienced before. Cold. Black. Slithering. Like an icy tentacle entwining itself in her brain.

Then slowly, without will, Marly lifted the gun to her temple.

And squeezed the trigger.

# Chapter Thirteen

The frantic knock on Deacon's door in the middle of the day startled him. The apparent urgency of whoever stood on the other side would have been more suited to a midnight visit, he thought as he drew back the door and received his second surprise.

Marly stood shivering on the landing, her hair and clothing drenched from the rain. But what stopped Deacon's heart was the look of terror in her eyes.

He took her arm and drew her inside the apartment. She came without resistance.

"What's the matter?" he asked anxiously. "What's happened?"

Her teeth were chattering so badly she couldn't speak. Deacon left her for a moment to fetch towels from the bathroom. When he came back, he gently helped her out of her jacket, then wrapped a towel around her shoulders and handed her another for her hair.

She went through the motions, blotting her hair and clothing as best she could, and by the time she was finished, she was able to speak. She still trembled, but the color had slowly returned to her face.

"Tell…me," she said.

"Tell you what?"

She closed her eyes briefly. "Tell me how to stop him."

"You believe me then." Deacon didn't know whether to be relieved or more worried than ever. What had finally convinced her? "What happened, Marly?"

She clutched the towel so tightly around her shoulders, her knuckles whitened. "He tried to kill me."

Her words sent a chill up Deacon's spine. Everything inside him went still with shock. Then rage. "When? Where?"

"Just a few minutes ago. I went over to Gracie Abbott's house to…check out something. A hunch. While I was there, someone came into her house." Marly turned from Deacon's gaze. "It sounds so crazy. I'm not even sure I can say it. But it happened." She ran a shaking hand through her hair. "I drew my weapon. The next thing I knew, the barrel was against my head. I could feel myself squeezing the trigger, but I couldn't stop," she whispered in horror. "That's how it must have been for all the others. They knew…they *knew*…but they couldn't stop it from happening."

She shuddered violently, and Deacon wanted nothing more than to pull her into his arms and hold her close, protect her from the evil that lurked somewhere outside his apartment. But his arms alone wouldn't shield her from the killer. Nothing would keep her safe except her own strength. And strength came from knowledge. From acceptance.

"Somehow I was able to let go of the gun. I don't know how or why. But I do know this." She lifted her desperate gaze to his. "It wasn't Sam."

"How can you be so sure?"

"Because I would have known," she said stubbornly. "I would have felt some kind of connection. And besides." Her eyes glittered with defiance, which Deacon took as a good sign. She was ready to fight back. "My brother would never hurt me."

*You weren't hurt,* Deacon started to remind her, but he held back. She'd been through enough. There would be time enough to hash out the suspects once he'd heard her whole story.

She drew a long breath. "Whoever he is, we have to find him. We have to stop him." She glanced up suddenly. "Can he be stopped?"

"He's human, if that's what you mean. He can be…neutralized," Deacon said.

"And that's where you come in." Her gaze faltered.

"Yes."

"Because…you're like him."

"Yes."

She clung to the towel. "You could kill me, right here and now and never lay a finger on me."

"I would never hurt you, Marly."

She didn't look altogether convinced on that point. "Just answer one question. Last night…was that you…did you make me—"

"I think you already know the answer to that question."

Turning, she walked over to the window to stare out. "How is any of this possible?"

"You want the long or short version?" he asked grimly.

She glanced over her shoulder. "Whatever it takes to make me understand."

He paused, searching for the right place to begin. "Do you know anything about quantum physics?"

"Only what I've seen on television." She shrugged. "I used to watch *Quantum Leap* when I was a kid."

"This goes way beyond a TV show," he said. "It even goes beyond mind control and psychokinesis. What I've told you so far is just the tip of the iceberg. The technology dates back to the end of the Second World War, when the experiments first went underground. Scientists and physicists connected to the project have been conducting experiments for years in psychotronics, particle beam technology, black hole simulation."

Marly turned. "What is psychotronics?"

"The interfacing of man and machine."

She put a hand to her mouth. "And black hole simulation? Particle beam technology?

"Time travel," he said. "Interdimensional phasing."

Her face had gone pale again. "My God. Do you have any idea how this sounds? How insane I feel just listening to you? You're spitting out terminology that I've never heard used outside of a science fiction movie.''

"This isn't fiction, Marly.'' He walked over to her. "It's reality. It's here and now, and we have to deal with it.''

"How? I'm just a small-town cop. I grew up in Mission Creek. I've barely even been out of the state of Texas. What you're telling me...is beyond my comprehension. How am I supposed to deal with something like that?''

He took her arm and drew her over to the sofa. When she was seated, he knelt in front of her. "You deal with it by hearing me out. By keeping an open mind. Knowledge is power.''

She moistened her lips. "I still don't know if I even trust you.''

"Then why did you come here?''

She glanced away. "Where else could I go?''

The anguish in her voice tore at Deacon's heart. He put a hand to her chin and gently turned her back to face him. "You can trust me, Marly. I'm one of the good guys.'' *Now.*

A myriad of emotions flashed across her features. "What are you?'' she finally asked. "Some kind of quantum cop?''

He almost smiled at that. "In a manner of speaking.'' He rose and began to pace. "The organization I work for is run by a man named Nicholas Kessler. Sixty years ago, he was a renowned scientist whose pioneer research into relativist and quantum physics attracted certain factions in the government that were searching for new and more innovative ways to combat the enemy. Dr. Kessler was commissioned to conduct a series of experiments involving electromagnetic fields on battleships. Ostensibly they were looking for an effective method to demagnetize the hulls of the ships so they would be invisible to enemy mines.''

Marly watched him from the sofa. She said nothing, but her eyes spoke volumes.

''What Dr. Kessler achieved instead was complete invisibility.''

She gasped. ''That's—''

''Impossible?'' Deacon's gaze met hers. ''Hear me out, remember? Keep an open mind.''

''I'm trying,'' she whispered.

''When the ship rematerialized, it seemed exactly as it was before, but the crew had undergone extreme physical and psychological trauma. Dr. Kessler was so distressed by the condition of the men that he tried to sabotage his own project in order to prevent the experiment from ever being repeated. He knew that if this new technology fell into the wrong hands, it could be catastrophic.''

Deacon walked over and sat down beside Marly. ''Unfortunately Dr. Kessler's notes had already been stolen by a group of rich and powerful men who operated underneath the radar of the government and even the intelligence community. They persuaded Dr. Kessler's protégé, a man named Joseph Von Meter, to continue the experiments in a series of underground bunkers at an abandoned Air Force station on Long Island, New York. Von Meter agreed, and to this day, he and Dr. Kessler remain bitter enemies.''

Marly glanced at him in surprise. "You mean...they're still alive?"

Deacon nodded. "They're old men, of course, but their rivalry is as strong as ever. As I said, Dr. Kessler runs the organization I work for. For the past sixty years, he's tried to put an end to what his own genius created. One of his primary goals is to find and, if necessary, eliminate the super soldiers created at Montauk."

"But you were—"

"I was one of them," Deacon agreed. "I underwent the experiments, the brainwashing, the mind control. I was trained to kill just like all the others."

Marly shuddered. "And you did so willingly, you said."

He nodded. "To a certain extent. But they'd been watching me for years. I excelled in both athletics and academics in school, and I even had a certain amount of psychic ability. They made it seem as if I'd volunteered to undergo the experiments, but I now believe that I was being prepared for the super soldier project at least as far back as high school."

"What about the others?"

He shrugged. "Some were like me. They were led into it gradually, subtly. Others were simply taken by force. When the experiments first started, they used mostly indigents. People who just disappeared off the streets and were never heard from again. Then they started to recruit military personnel and eventually they began to use children. Some of them came from military families, but they also used bogus child-care facilities and phony cults as a means to screen suitable subjects.''

''What did they do to them?'' Marly's expression revealed the revulsion she felt for everything he'd told her.

Deacon knew exactly how she felt. He'd had a hard time accepting the truth, too. Especially his part in it. ''I didn't find out about the children until much later, but from everything I've learned since, even the youngest were put through rigorous training and brainwashing techniques until they became adept at whatever special ability they showed an aptitude for. Then their memories were erased. The objective was to send them back home or back out into society until such time as they were needed.''

Marly lifted her gaze. ''An army of secret warriors,'' she whispered in horror.

''WHAT WERE THE EXPERIMENTS like?'' she asked a little while later as she watched Deacon move about the tiny kitchen, making coffee for himself and a cup of tea for her.

He carried the steaming mugs to the table and sat down across from her. ''Some of them were pretty brutal. I didn't personally witness any physical abuse, but I do know they used fear and sleep deprivation as a means to control the subjects. The goal was to dissociate and compartmentalize the mind and personality. For me, it started off with various hypnosis techniques where I learned the process of deep relaxation, visualization and, to a lesser extent, self-healing. From there, I progressed into simple telekinesis. Bending spoons, etc. Eventually I learned to manipulate basic psychological states, interfere with coherent mental functioning and motor reflexes, interface with both conscious and subconscious thought processes, and plant subliminal messages.''

Marly thought back to that day when she'd stood on Ricky Morales's porch. She could have sworn she'd heard music coming from inside his house, but at the same time, she'd somehow known it was only in her head. Had that been a subliminal message? Had Ricky's killer even then been sending her a clue?

"You said the project was shut down. Why?"

He took a sip of his coffee and grimaced. "The project had been underground ever since World War Two. Private funding allowed them to operate beneath the government's radar, but after the submarine accident, I think things probably got a little dicey. It's hard to cover up something of that magnitude. Certain people became suspicious and too many questions were being asked. They abandoned the Montauk facility, but we figure they had other locations. If they haven't already started back up somewhere else, they will. You can't keep Pandora's Box closed forever.''

Marly was silent for a moment, trying to take it all in. "You have no idea why you were on board that submarine?"

"No." He stared down at his coffee. "Like I said, we were to be briefed only when we reached the drop zone. But my feeling is that it was something big. Something that made even the scientists in charge of the project nervous. That's why they were so quick to shut down the whole operation when it failed.''

Marly wrapped her fingers around her cup, letting the warmth chase away her lingering chill. "How did you hook up with this Dr. Kessler?"

"I met his granddaughter first. I thought it was a chance meeting, but I've since come to believe that nothing in my life has ever been left to fate."

Marly shivered at the sudden darkness in his eyes. "That must have been a terrifying revelation," she said softly. "But at least you're aware of the manipulation now. At least you can fight it."

"You know something about that, don't you?" Their gazes met, and Marly had the strangest sensation of déjà vu, as if she and Deacon had met before, in another time, another life. Once she might have laughed at such a fantasy, but after today, she couldn't dismiss any possibility.

"Go on," she said. "I want to hear the rest."

He shrugged, dropping his gaze back to his coffee. "After the accident, they wiped out our memories before we were cut loose, but I had just enough recall to know that I didn't have any close family, no one to go home to. I did have a bank account, though, enough to get by on for quite a while if I was careful. So I more or less bummed around the country, picking up jobs here and there. I even drove out to California, although I still don't really know why. I think that's where I grew up. Anyway, I was in a convenience store in East L.A. one day when a man rushed in armed with an automatic weapon. There were two other customers in the store besides me. Two women and a little boy.

"The gunman shot the clerk and grabbed the kid to use as a hostage. I knew it was going to end badly. I knew that little boy was going to die. We all were. I could see it in the gunman's eyes. So I made him turn the weapon on himself and pull the trigger. That was the first time I realized what I could do. I wasn't even aware I possessed the ability until that day."

Marly's heart was beating a painful staccato inside her chest. She didn't know how or why, but she felt as if she'd been in that store with Deacon. She felt as if she'd witnessed every second of the tableau he'd just described.

"You saved that little boy's life."

He looked up. "I also took a life. And I knew I'd done it before because it came too easy for me."

Their gazes held for a moment, and Marly shuddered at what she saw in his eyes. The pain and anguish. The memories of death.

Impulsively she reached across the table and placed her hand on his. "You did what you had to do, Deacon."

It was the first time she'd used his given name, and Marly felt a thrill of excitement race up her spine. Whether it was from the sound of his name or the physical contact, she didn't know. But something was drawing them closer. Pulling them inexorably together.

Abruptly she released his hand and clasped her own in her lap. "What happened after that?"

"Nothing happened to me. The police thought the man had panicked and committed suicide when he realized there was no way out. I let them believe that and walked away. It was only later that I found out someone was on to me."

"Kessler's granddaughter?"

"She was one of the women in the store that day. Not the kid's mother, but the other one. I'd noticed her when she first walked in. Dark hair. Blue eyes. A real knockout. There was something familiar about her, too, but I couldn't place where I'd seen her before. Then afterward, I saw her watching me. She had a strange look on her face, as if she knew what I'd done. I didn't give it much thought at the time. I was still pretty shaken by what had happened. What I had made happen.

"A few days later, she came to see me. She said she knew who I was and what I could do."

Marly lifted a brow. "And?"

"She said there was someone who wanted to meet me."

Marly stared at him for a moment. "And you agreed? Just like that? Not even knowing who she was?" *Dark hair. Blue eyes. A real knockout.* Men could be so stupid.

"She piqued my curiosity," Deacon said a little defensively. "Besides, I figured I didn't have much to lose."

"Does this woman have a name?" Marly tried to ask casually.

"Camille."

*Camille.* It would have to be something exotic. *Dark hair. Blue eyes. A real knockout.* The kind of woman men would follow anywhere.

The kind of woman that was the exact opposite of Marly. She'd never held any delusions about her own sex appeal. She was a mildly attractive woman who'd never excelled at anything in her life. Not athletics. Not academics. She wasn't even a very good cop. And most telling of all, she hadn't been able to keep her fiancé from straying.

"What did they want with you?" she couldn't help asking.

"At first, they were mostly interested in the submarine accident and what I knew about the mission. They'd already determined that each member of the special ops team on board was carefully screened and selected because he was an expert at one or more psionic skills. Dr. Kessler believed, and still does, that if and when Montauk regroups, they might try and repeat the mission. And if they do, they may also try to resurrect the same team."

"So, as a preemptive strike, they recruited you to their side," Marly said.

He nodded. "At first, I reacted to everything they told me the same way you did. I thought it was some kind of scam. It sounded too far-fetched to be true, and yet I knew what I could do. I knew the psychokinesis wasn't normal. I'd been trained to do it. Programmed to do it. And I also knew that if I'd been able to kill that man in the store so easily, there was a good chance I might do so again. And maybe the next time my reason wouldn't be so noble.''

"SO HOW DO WE FIND HIM?''

They were still seated at the table and Deacon was on his second cup of coffee. He wondered how Marly was handling everything he'd told her. She seemed okay. The hand that lifted the tea to her lips was almost steady.

Deacon set aside his own cup and folded his arms on the table. "We use the profile. From there it's a process of elimination.''

"Yes, well, I have a little problem with that profile.'' Marly carefully returned her cup to the table. "You think the killer is someone between the ages of thirty and forty. But from what you just told me, these experiments have been going on for years. How do you know the killer isn't someone older?''

"Because we're working in the time frame of when the super soldier project escalated,'' Deacon said. "It's not exact, that's for sure. But it's a place to start.''

"You also said that the subjects were mostly male. Mostly, but not all, right? The killer could conceivably be a woman.''

"I suppose it's possible,'' Deacon agreed. "There were a few women in the project. The only one I personally know of was taken when she was five years old. Her father was a scientist who worked for Von Meter, and the girl was abducted to keep the father in line. They ended up holding her for over four years,'' he said grimly.

"And when she was released, could she control thoughts?" Marly asked.

"No. She could walk through walls."

Marly opened her mouth to say something, then shook her head. "Nothing should surprise me anymore," she muttered. She toyed with her cup before glancing up. "Supposing you're right. Supposing the killer does fit the profile. That doesn't mean Sam is the one. There are a lot of other people in this town who meet the same criteria."

Deacon studied her for a moment. "You have someone in mind?"

She shrugged. "When Navarro first came to town, there were rumors that he was an ex-Navy SEAL. He's also the right age."

"And you still think it strange that he didn't mention his conversation with Lisa Potter."

Marly nodded. "Among other things. In spite of all that, though, I don't really think he's a killer. But there is someone else in town I get strange vibes from."

"Who?"

She hesitated. "Joshua Rush."

Deacon lifted a brow.

"I know, I know," Marly said quickly. "You're probably thinking this is some sort of personal vendetta, but it's not. Even when we were…together, there was something about him that I found very unsettling. His intensity could be almost frightening at times. We were only engaged for a couple of weeks, but I knew right from the start that I'd made a terrible mistake. Even if I hadn't caught him with another woman, I would have found a way to break things off with him. I would never have married that man.''

''I believe you,'' Deacon said.

Marly tucked her still damp hair behind her ears. ''Something you said earlier got me to thinking. They used cults to screen potential subjects. What if the killer was recruited or even taken by force from one of those cults? When his mind was erased and he was cut loose, wouldn't he have returned to what he knew?''

''To a cult, you mean.''

''Or something close to it.'' Marly folded her arms on the table and leaned toward Deacon. ''There's something very cultlike about the Glorious Way Church. At least there is since Joshua came here. You have to see the way he is with his congregation. Or more to the point, the way they are with him. It's like he has some kind of hold on them.''

''Any chance you can arrange for us to have a little chat with Reverend Rush?''

''I'll do better than that,'' Marly said grimly. ''They're holding church services every night this week. I'll take you to see him in action.''

## Chapter Fourteen

By the time Marly and Deacon arrived at the Glorious Way Church that night, the revival meeting was in full swing and the place was packed. Joshua had to love that, Marly thought dryly. He always enjoyed playing to a full house.

He was just getting warmed up, but already he had them eating out of his hand. The crowd was so captivated that no one seemed to notice when Marly and Deacon slipped in and took seats at the back.

Marly scanned the chapel. Most of the congregation had their backs to her, but some were in profile as they turned to gaze up at the pulpit. She recognized several people in attendance. A couple from her apartment complex. A man she'd stopped for speeding a week or so ago. A deputy and his wife.

Her gaze lit on a dark-haired man seated at the end of a pew several rows up. Even from the back, there was something familiar about him, but Marly wasn't sure why. Then, as if sensing her scrutiny, he turned and glanced over his shoulder.

When their gazes met, Max Perry smiled and nodded, then returned his attention to the pulpit. But in that brief instance, Marly felt the glimmer of something that might have been a premonition.

What was he doing here? she wondered. He didn't strike her as the churchgoing type, but then Marly knew very little about him. For all she knew, he was here because of the community outreach program. Perhaps he'd been invited to speak, but somehow Marly doubted that even the deaths of four people could persuade Joshua Rush to share the limelight.

Her gaze shifted to the front pew, and suddenly she forgot all about Max Perry as a chill raced up her backbone. Her mother's face was in profile, but Marly had no trouble discerning her expression as she stared up at Joshua. She looked enraptured. Enthralled. In love.

And Marly felt sick.

"Are you okay?" Deacon said in her ear.

She turned. "What?"

He glanced down where her hands clutched the edge of the pew so tightly her knuckles whitened. "You're holding on as if you're afraid you might lift off from that seat."

"I'm fine," she said, although she was far from fine.

"Where does that corridor lead?" Deacon whispered. He nodded to the side of the chapel where an archway opened into a narrow corridor that led back into the building.

"To the offices and Sunday school rooms," she said. "Why?"

"Where is Rush's office?"

"All the way back."

When Deacon started to get up, Marly caught his arm. "Where are you going?"

"To have a look around."

Her grip tightened. "What if someone sees you?"

His gaze roamed over the crowd. "Do you really think anyone will notice?"

Marly followed his gaze. And shivered. There was something deeply unnerving about all those faces gazing so raptly at Joshua.

"Are you coming?" Deacon asked in ear.

"In a minute," she whispered back.

He nodded, then slipped away. Marly remained seated, her gaze sweeping over the congregation to make sure his departure hadn't attracted attention. But all eyes remained focused on Joshua.

By now he was really hitting his stride. Armed with a cordless microphone, he left the pulpit to roam among his followers, shaking hands, squeezing shoulders, embracing. When he came to Marly's mother, he skimmed her cheek with his fingers. Andrea Jessop caught his hand in hers and lifted it to her lips.

Marly's heart did a nosedive. She was shocked by such an open display of affection between her mother and her ex-fiancé. However, no one else seemed to notice. Or care.

But Marly cared. Not because she was jealous. Not because she still had feelings for Joshua. But because she knew her mother would end up getting hurt.

Getting to her feet, Marly slipped along the back

of the pew to the arched doorway. She didn't even turn to see if anyone had noticed her departure. At that point, she wasn't sure she even cared.

Heading straight for the ladies' room, she leaned over one of the sinks and splashed cold water on her face until her queasy stomach began to settle. She turned off the tap, and just as she was reaching for a paper towel, the lights went out. Everything was suddenly pitch-black.

Marly remained motionless, trying to orient herself to the darkness. She wanted to believe the whole church was experiencing a power outage, but she didn't think that was the case. Someone had turned off the lights in the bathroom. Someone, perhaps, who had followed Marly out of the chapel.

She knew that she could make her way across the room to the exit with very little trouble, but she also knew that if she drew back the door, there was a good chance the killer would be waiting on the other side. If she were a braver person, she would have done exactly that, Marly thought. Find out once and for all who was responsible for all these deaths.

But after the episode at Miss Gracie's house, she now knew exactly what she was dealing with. Even armed, she was no match for the killer. Her only hope was Deacon.

As efficiently as she could manage, Marly groped her way across the floor to the bathroom stalls. Feeling her way along the metal doors, she entered the one farthest from the exit and shot home the bolt.

He would find her. Marly knew that. It wouldn't

take any special powers to figure out where she was hiding. But what else could she do?

Leaning against the wall, she listened to the darkness. And then, a moment later, the bathroom door creaked open.

He was out there. Only a few feet from where she stood. He was out there and he was going to kill her.

No, that wasn't right. He was going to make her kill herself. Everyone would think her death another suicide. Everyone except Deacon.

Deacon. Where was he? Oh, God, if only she had his power. If only she could make things happen with her mind. If only he could find her in time—

The door on the stall at the far end slammed shut, and Marly jumped, pressing her hand to her mouth to smother the scream that bubbled in her throat.

Another door slammed.

Then another.

There were five stalls in the rest room. Marly was in the last one. She realized in horror what he was doing. He was working his way down to her.

The door next to her opened and banged shut so violently that a gasp escaped through Marly's fingers. Then suddenly all the doors began to slam so fast and so furiously that Marly couldn't hold back a scream. The door to her own stall rattled and shook, but the killer didn't open the door. He didn't even try to invade her mind. It was different this time. Somehow Marly knew that he had no intention of actually harming her. He merely wanted her to experience—and appreciate—his rage and frustration.

After a moment, the cacophony subsided, and everything was silent again. The bathroom door opened and closed, and Marly knew that he was gone. But she didn't come out of the stall. She didn't even release her breath until the lights came back on, and she heard Deacon call out her name.

Then her knees gave way, and she slid trembling to the floor.

DEACON PULLED INTO A PARKING space outside Marly's apartment and killed the engine. "Maybe it would be a good idea if I bunked at your place tonight. I don't think you should be alone."

Marly didn't think having Deacon spend the night was such a hot idea, either. She was in a vulnerable state at the moment, but she nodded in agreement because she didn't want to be alone. After tonight, there was no question in her mind that she was vulnerable to the killer. He'd targeted her, but for what purpose, she still had no idea.

Letting them into the apartment, she turned on lights, then headed for the refrigerator. "I'm having a glass of wine," she said. "Which is the strongest thing I've got. Care to join me?"

"Sure, why not?"

Marly poured two glasses and brought them and the bottle back out to the living area. Handing one of the wineglasses to Deacon, she motioned to the sofa, then took a seat across from him on an armchair. Lifting the glass to her lips, she polished off the contents in two gulps.

"Whoa," Deacon said. "Maybe you should take it a little easy with that."

"I probably should," Marly agreed. "But in case you missed it, I've had a pretty rough day. Two run-ins with a psychic killer is a little more excitement than I'm used to." She poured herself another glass. "But it was different tonight. *He* was different," she mused with a frown. "He scared the hell out of me, but I don't think he ever intended to hurt me. It was more like he was…letting me see his frustration."

Deacon frowned. "His frustration?"

"I know that sounds crazy." Marly took another drink of wine. "But that's the impression I got. What I don't understand is why he's chosen me."

"I can think of a couple of reasons. It's not un-usual for a serial killer to make contact with the police, even to seek out one cop in particular. He sends messages, he taunts, he even fancies he has a relationship with that cop."

Marly glanced up. "You think that's what's going on here?"

"Could be. Or it could be someone who feels, rightly or wrongly, that he already has a relationship with you." Deacon paused. "Each time he's made contact, have you been able to pick up anything, no matter how subtle, that might give us a clue to his identity?"

"Not really. Although—" Marly leaned forward to place her glass on the coffee table. "Are you familiar with a song called 'Gloomy Sunday?'"

He shook his head.

"That song was playing the day I found my grandmother. I heard it the moment I walked into the house. It was what…led me upstairs to the body. I even used to have nightmares about it. The other day at Ricky Morales's house…I thought I heard it again, but I decided it must have been my imagination. Something had triggered a memory for me. But that same evening, I drove out to Old Cemetery Road where Amber's and David's bodies were found. I had the strangest feeling that someone was watching me. Then I found myself humming 'Gloomy Sunday' as if—'' She broke off.

"As if someone had planted it in your head?"

"I know what you're thinking," she said defensively. "You think that if the killer is sending me some kind of message with that song, he has to be someone who knows me. Someone close to me. But it could be just a coincidence. 'Gloomy Sunday' is called the suicide song. It's one of those urban legends that even has Web sites devoted to it. Anyone could have found out about it."

"Did Sam know about that song, Marly?"

She stared down at her wineglass. "He was the first one to arrive after my frantic phone call that day. He went up to…make sure Grandmother was dead while I waited on the porch. So I assume he heard the song. And if he didn't turn off the phonograph, then my parents and the police heard it, as well. At any rate, I told them about it when I gave my statement. Anyone who has access to the police department's records and archives could have learned about that song. And, besides, Mission Creek is a small town. People talk. Words gets around.''

''Did you ever tell anyone about it?''

''No, I don't think so. It wasn't something I liked to talk about. But I can't speak for anyone else who was at my grandmother's that day. I do know that Sam and Max Perry have become good friends. If they got to talking about the recent suicides, I suppose it'd be natural for Sam to mention what happened to our grandmother in the course of the conversation.''

Deacon lifted his glass, his gaze meeting Marly's over the rim. ''You didn't even tell Joshua Rush?''

''No...but someone else may have.''

''Who?''

''My mother has started going to the Glorious Way Church. I saw her there tonight.''

He looked surprised. ''Was that why you were so upset?''

She nodded. ''According to my father, she and Joshua have become...close.''

''How close?''

Marly sighed. ''I don't know.''

''Does the possibility of a relationship between them bother you?''

''Not in the way you mean. I just don't want to see my mother get hurt. She's been through so much with my father.''

''She's a grown woman, Marly. She has a right to make her own mistakes.''

"I know that." Marly tucked her hair behind her ears. "It's just…"

"You don't want to see her end up with another man like your father. You don't want that for yourself, either, do you?" he asked softly.

Marly scowled. "What are you getting at?"

Deacon shrugged. "You've erected some pretty damn thick walls, Marly. I wonder if you'll ever let anyone inside."

Her frown deepened as she glared at him across the coffee table. "Look who's talking?"

"Meaning?"

"You've convinced yourself that you did terrible things because you were able to kill a man, without much effort, in order to save a little boy's life. But you don't even remember if you were a killer or not. You assume you were because…that's what you were trained to do. But true or not, it's a good excuse to keep everyone at arm's length, isn't it?" Marly leaned toward him. "You know what I think? I think you've got your own walls. I think you're afraid of getting hurt."

Something glinted in his eyes. "Are you saying you and I have something in common, Marly?"

His look sent a shiver up her spine. "Not really. How could we? You've experienced things I can't even comprehend. I'm just a simple small town girl. I grew up in Mission Creek. I've barely even been out of Texas."

He was still looking at her, still making her shiver. "You could change all that."

"I don't know." She ran a finger around the rim of her wineglass. "It's a scary world out there."

"Scarier than Mission Creek?"

Her gaze lifted to meet his. "Good point," she said with a shudder.

AFTER THREE GLASSES OF WINE, Marly had finally begun to relax. To mellow, even. And suddenly it didn't seem like such a mistake after all to have Deacon spend the night. It had been a long time since she'd enjoyed a man's company. And Deacon wasn't just any man. He was handsome and fascinating and...scary. Marly was nervous just being in the same room with him.

But trying not to show it, she got up and took the empty wine bottle and glasses into the kitchen. "The bathroom's just down the hallway," she said over her shoulder. "There should be plenty of fresh towels, and I think there's even a new toothbrush in the top drawer of the vanity."

"New toothbrush, huh?"

She turned at that. "I know what you're thinking, but I don't make a habit of inviting people to spend the night. Especially not...strangers." Not handsome, fascinating, scary strangers anyway. "I always buy more than one toothbrush at a time."

"Very efficient," he remarked. His gaze said something else. There was suddenly a lot of tension in her small apartment, Marly realized. Sexual and otherwise. She'd never been so aware of a man's presence before. Was she ready for this? Ready to finish what Deacon's eyes had started?

She moistened her lips. "Yes, that's me. I'm practical through and through." And it was high time the practical Marly reasserted herself. "I'll get you some bedding."

"Just toss me a blanket," Deacon said. "I don't need much in the way of creature comforts."

No? Then what did he need? "You'll need a decent place to sleep." She hauled out sheets, pillows and blankets. "Otherwise, you won't get much rest."

"I doubt I'll sleep much tonight anyway."

His voice sent a whispery thrill along Marly's already jagged nerve endings. "Why not?" she asked, her own voice suddenly breathless.

"I'm here to protect you, remember?"

Oh. Marly fought down her disappointment, and maybe just a little relief, as she bent to make up the sofa. Deacon tried to help her, but somehow their arms became entangled, and shivering from the contact, Marly straightened.

Deacon straightened.

For the longest moment, they stared into each other's eyes. Then slowly Deacon lifted a hand to smooth back her hair.

Marly bit her lip. "This probably isn't a good idea."

"I'm pretty sure it's not."

"Then why—"

His gaze darkened, warmed. "Because I've wanted to do this all night."

"Do what—" But her question was cut off when he bent and pressed his lips to hers. And suddenly,

Marly forgot what she'd been about to ask. Forgot everything except the feel of Deacon's mouth on hers.

She wrapped her arms around his neck and kissed him back, eagerly, passionately, wholeheartedly, and the next thing she knew, he had her up against a wall, touching her in places that had her gasping for breath.

And then they turned, and she pressed him into the wall, kissing him so deeply that he groaned against her mouth. And deepened the kiss.

They kissed all the way down the hallway to the bedroom, stumbling and falling against the wall in their urgency. By the time they reached Marly's bedroom, she was completely naked.

On the rare occasions she'd found herself in similar situations, she'd felt awkward and humbled and horribly self-conscious. With Deacon she felt brave and beautiful and womanly.

And he was certainly all man. Every glorious…inch of him. Marly caught her breath as he shrugged out of his clothes and stood before her in the moonlight.

She couldn't believe…

She'd never imagine…not in her wildest dreams…

"My God," she breathed just before he swept her up and carried her off to bed.

She lay on her back, and he rose over her, his eyes burning into hers. "You're a gorgeous woman, Marly Jessop." His gaze swept over her. "You look exactly the way I imagined you."

"You...imagined me like this?"

"Only since the moment I first laid eyes on you."
And then his hands and mouth went to work, weaving their incredible magic. He touched her in places that Marly had never considered particularly erogenous, but with Deacon, the skim of his tongue against the back of her knee, the trace of his fingertip along the lines of her palm became unbearably sensual.

Marly began to tremble. They'd barely gotten started and already she felt out of control. With an effort, she rolled Deacon off her, then straddled him so that she could work a little magic of her own.

When he tried to protest, she merely smiled.

THAT SMILE. That smile was going to be the end of him, Deacon thought. It was all sweet and innocent, and yet there was a bad girl lurking in there somewhere. A passionate, fascinating woman just waiting to get sprung. And he was doing his damnedest to free her.

Marly had been wrong earlier. She wasn't a simple small town girl. She wasn't a simple anything. She was complicated and confusing and dangerous. Deacon had never known anyone like her. Never known anyone whose outer persona was in such contradiction to her true inner self.

He was seeing a bit of the real Marly now as she bent to kiss him. As she did to him exactly what he'd done to her. Her hands explored. Her mouth grazed...and lingered, and in a moment, Deacon knew that he would be the one out of control. He didn't want that to happen. Not yet. There was still so much of Marly to experience. To savor. To…cherish.

He pulled her to him, but when he would have taken charge, she resisted by entwining her fingers with his and lifting his arms over his head as she kissed him so deeply he could hardly breathe.

"I'm the one in control," she murmured against his mouth. "Understood?"

"Perfectly," he whispered.

"I can do to you whatever I want, right?"

"The sooner the better," he agreed.

She smiled down at him again, but this time, all sweetness and innocence were gone. The real Marly had finally come out to play.

*Chapter Fifteen*

Marly lifted her head and squinted at the sunshine streaming in through her bedroom window. She knew instantly that something was different about this morning. She was naked, for one thing, and she never slept in the nude. And then there were the sheets, all tangled around her legs and her head was cushioned on Deacon's hip.

Nope, not a normal morning at all.

Deacon was covered by the rumpled sheet, thank goodness, but still, Marly had never awakened in such a compromising position. When she moved away from temptation, Deacon stirred but didn't wake up.

She lay for a moment staring at the ceiling as her fuzzy memory began to clear and everything came back to her. Every touch, every kiss, every word that had been uttered between them in the heat of passion. And they'd said a lot. They'd done things that Marly…

She couldn't believe how bold she'd been. How aggressive. How…creative. She couldn't believe that she'd allowed herself to be that open and free with anyone, and there could only be one explanation for it.

That hadn't been her.

That wasn't the real Marly.

That hedonistic creature last night had undoubtedly been the woman of Deacon's fantasies, and he'd made those fantasies come true by getting inside Marly's head, by manipulating her into saying and doing things she never would have on her own.

In the dark of night, Deacon had made her want him as she'd never wanted a man in her life, made her behave in a way Marly never would have thought herself capable. And now in the light of day, she couldn't help feeling betrayed. Used. Violated.

A strong sentiment, she realized, and maybe she was overreacting a little. But Marly couldn't stand the thought of someone having that kind of power over her. It was terrifying.

As quietly as she could, she rose from bed and grabbed a clean uniform from her closet and fresh underwear from her bureau, then headed off to the shower. Locking herself in the bathroom, she turned on the taps and stood under the hot spray for as long as she could stand. When she finally came out of the bathroom, all dressed and ready for work, Deacon was up and around. Wearing only his jeans, he stood at the window staring out until he heard Marly approach and then he turned with a smile.

And Marly's knees went all weak in spite of her resolve.

DEACON COULD TELL SOMETHING was wrong the moment he saw Marly in the doorway. She didn't return his smile, nor would she meet his gaze.

He walked across the room toward her. "You look like a woman who's suffering from a bad case of regrets."

His light tone did nothing to restore her humor. She folded her arms and stared up at him. "Regrets? Yeah, you might say that."

"Why?"

"Why?" Her tone was laced with resentment. "Because that woman you were in bed with last night wasn't me."

Deacon frowned. "What are you talking about?"

"You know damn well what I'm talking about." She unfolded her arms and moved past him to the window. But she only spent a moment gazing at the view before she spun to face him. "You made me...that way."

Deacon could hardly believe what he was hearing. Surely she didn't think...

But obviously she did. She'd managed to convince herself that last night had been all his doing. Nothing like a little finger-pointing to get the morning after started off in the right direction. His own voice deepened with anger. "Look, Marly. It was two consenting adults in that bed last night. Let's not kid ourselves about that."

He saw her glance at the bed before she quickly looked away. Lifting her chin, she said, "That's the trouble. I don't know that I did consent."

He ran his hand through his hair as he stared back at her. "This is crazy. I didn't make you do anything you didn't want to do.'' That she hadn't been *eager* to do, but he didn't think it was a good time to bring that up.

''Yes, well, that's the whole point. How do I know you didn't make me want it? You've been inside my head before. How do I know you weren't there again last night? How do I know you weren't manipulating me? And if you were, I gotta say, that was a pretty nasty thing to do. You might as well have raped me.'' She spat out the word so angrily, so full of contempt, that Deacon reeled from the shock. She couldn't have stunned him more had she slapped him across the face.

''*Raped* you? My God, Marly, is that really what you think? Because that's a pretty ugly accusation. You sure that's what you mean?''

She glanced away. ''Maybe that is too strong,'' she relented. ''Maybe I am overreacting. But if you did something to me—''

''I didn't. What we did last night was what a man and woman do when they're attracted to each other. It's natural.''

Her face turned beet red. ''No, what we did was—''

''Out of control? That's the real problem, isn't it, Marly?'' He took a step or two toward her. ''What is your real concern here? You're not so much worried that I got inside your head and manipulated your thoughts as you're afraid that the real Marly revealed herself last night. You were passionate and needy and vulnerable…and that scares you, doesn't it?''

''You don't know what you're talking about.'' But her words held no real conviction, and Deacon knew that he was hitting a little too close to home for her.

''You can't accept who you really are, can you?'' he demanded softly. ''Is that really how you want to live your life? Hiding behind those walls so you don't end up like your mother?''

''If that's what it takes,'' she said stubbornly. ''Besides, why do you care? You'll be gone from here soon. We'll never see each other again. Last night was just a…one-night stand. Why do you care how I live my life?''

His gaze softened. ''Because I care about you.''

''I don't want you to care.''

Too late for that, Deacon thought. He already cared far too much. He cared so much that he was in danger of getting in way over his head here.

Because Marly was right about one thing. He had no business caring about her. He had nothing to offer a woman like her. He had a job to do and a past to make up for. He couldn't settle down in Mission Creek, and he certainly couldn't ask Marly to be a part of his life. Because he had no life. Not anymore.

He was a man without a home, a man without memories. He was a soldier who'd been programmed to kill—and might do so again someday.

It was better that Marly not trust him. It was better that she kept her distance because Deacon didn't even trust himself.

"Okay, you're right," he said, trying to ignore the hollow feeling in his stomach, the emptiness inside his heart. "I made last night happen."

She put a trembling hand to her mouth. "Oh, my God."

"Marly, I'm sorry—"

When he started toward her, she backed away from him, her eyes blazing with fury. But behind that anger was a hurt and betrayal that tore at Deacon's resolve. "Get out," she whispered. "Get the hell out of my apartment."

Deacon turned, and without another word, walked away.

AFTER BEING ON PATROL for most of the day, Marly decided to take a break that afternoon and swing by the school to see Sam. Not that she planned to unburden herself to him or anything. She and Sam were close these days, but there were still some things a sister couldn't tell a brother, and her night with Deacon Cage was one of them.

All day long, Marly had tried to convince herself that what had happened between her and Deacon was no big deal. People had one-night stands all the time. But she didn't. She'd never been able to take sex that casually until Deacon had made her—

Marly shook her head, determined not to think about it anymore. Determined not to dwell on what just might be the biggest betrayal of her life.

Funny how even catching her own fiancé in bed with another woman hadn't affected her so deeply. Hadn't hurt her this badly. In fact, after her initial anger and disgust wore off, Marly had been secretly relieved because it had given her the perfect excuse to break things off.

But what Deacon had done...

Marly knew she wasn't going to get over that for a very long time. He'd tapped into her worst fear and used it against her. That was unforgivable, especially considering that she had begun to suspect there was more than attraction between them. She had even started to care for him, maybe even to fall for him a little, but that was over with now. Marly never wanted to see him again.

All she wanted to do now was talk to her brother. After seeing Max Perry at church the evening before, Marly was starting to get a strange feeling about the high school counselor, and she wanted to ask Sam a few questions about the man's past. After all, she knew nothing about Max and he just happened to fit the killer's profile, at least age-wise. And the more Marly thought about it, the more she wondered if Sam might have mentioned details of their grandmother's suicide to Max. Details like "Gloomy Sunday."

It was a long shot, but Marly no longer had any doubt that something very sinister was going on in Mission Creek. She'd seen too many things, *felt* too many things, that couldn't be explained away.

Pulling into a parking space at the front of the school, Marly got out and headed up the sidewalk. Following school policy, she went by the office before heading back to Sam's classroom.

A young woman carrying an armload of papers

dashed into the office right behind Marly. She took one look at Marly's uniform and stopped in her tracks, her face going pale. "Oh, no. What happened? Why are you here?"

"I'm just here to see my brother," Marly explained. "Sam Jessop?"

The young woman let out a long sigh of relief. "Oh, thank goodness." She walked around the counter and dropped down into a chair where she began to fan herself with one of the papers. "You'll have to excuse me, but it's been a crazy morning around here. We're shorthanded and Mr. Henesey is on a real tear. He should just fire that woman and be done with it, but it's not my place to say anything—" She caught herself and glanced up. "Sorry. Mr. Jessop, you say?" She tapped a few keys on her computer. "Oh. He's not here today."

"Not here," Marly repeated. "Did he call in sick?"

"No, it says here he's taking a personal leave day. Did you want to leave a message or anything?"

"No, I'll just catch him later. Thanks anyway." Marly started to turn away, then paused. "What about Max Perry?"

"I saw him just a little while ago, but I don't know if he was heading back to his office or not. I can page him if you like."

"No, don't bother," Marly said. "I'll just stick my head in his office and see if he's there."

"Go down the hall and make a right. It's the first door on your right."

"Thanks."

Marly had no trouble locating the door marked
Counselor, but Max wasn't inside. She glanced over
her shoulder, making sure no one was about. She
could just have a quick look and be on her way
before anyone was the wiser.

Hurrying over to Max's desk, she gazed down at
the assortment of folders and reports scattered across
the top. She had no idea what she was looking for.
She had no real reason to suspect Max Perry of anything except that shortly after she'd seen him at the
Glorious Way last night, the killer had followed her
into the bathroom.

Didn't mean that Max was guilty, she reminded
herself as she thumbed through his desk calendar. A
few pages back, a notation at the bottom stopped
her. Marly stared at it for a moment, frowning.
*Meeting AT* was all it said.

Meeting at? Marly wondered. Or Meeting A.T.?

A.T.

Amber Tyson.

Marly quickly glanced at the date at the top of
the page. It was the day Amber and David had died.

Voices sounded from the hallway and Marly
quickly flipped the calendar back to the current date.
Then grabbing pad and pen, she began to scribble a
note.

By the time Max walked through his door, she
was able to glance up and say quite convincingly,
"Oh, hey, Max. I was just leaving you a note."

His gaze narrowed a bit before he said cheerily,
"Marly! This is a surprise. What are you doing
here?"

She straightened and came around the desk, putting herself between Max and the doorway. "Phil Garner called the station. He wants to know if we're interested in doing his show again next week."

"Hmm. I'll have to check my schedule." Max walked over to his desk and glanced down at his calendar. Marly's heart skipped a beat. Had she returned it to the proper day?

"He didn't mention a particular day," she said quickly. "I'll have to get back to you on that."

Max glanced up. "That's fine. But you didn't have to drive all the way over here for that. You could have called and left a message."

Marly tucked a stray twig of hair behind her ears. "Oh, I know. I wanted to see Sam anyway, but the receptionist told me that he's not here today."

Max scowled. "He's not? I saw him last night. He didn't say anything about feeling under the weather."

When had he seen Sam? Before or after he'd attended the service at the Glorious Way?

"I'm sure it's nothing serious," Marly said. "Maybe he just needed a day off. Don't we all?" she added.

He gave her a quick once-over. "Are you feeling okay?"

Marly shrugged. "I'm fine. Why do you ask?"

"You seem a little…tense today."

Marly couldn't imagine why. She was chasing an elusive killer who offed people with his mind. She'd slept with a man the night before who'd turned her into a woman she didn't even recognize. And in spite of the way he'd manipulated her, *violated* her, Marly still couldn't get him out of her head.

Tense? That was an understatement. "I'm just a little tired. It's pretty hectic at the station these days. Someone's kid doesn't make it home in time for dinner, the parents call the station, frantic because they're sure something terrible has happened. Everyone in town is on edge."

Max toyed with a pencil on his desk. "This has to be especially hard for you."

"Why do you say that?"

He bounced the rubber eraser off the desktop. "Sam told me about your grandmother. That's a pretty traumatic thing for a twelve-year-old kid to go through. He said you had nightmares about it for a long time afterward."

For a moment, Marly was mesmerized by the movement of the pencil. Then she glanced up, meeting Max's gaze. There was something in his eyes…

Or was that her imagination? Marly tried to pull her attention back to the conversation.

"He says he sometimes still has nightmares about it," Max said softly.

Marly moistened her lips. She was starting to get a bad feeling about this conversation, as if Max was purposefully feeding her information to pique her curiosity. Or to taunt her.

"Sam still has nightmares? Then why in the world did he move into Grandmother's house?"

The pencil eraser bounced again. "Maybe he thought he could exorcise some old ghosts."

"Maybe." Marly hesitated. "Did he tell you any of the details of her death?"

"Enough that I have a pretty clear picture of what you must have seen. She hanged herself, right?" Bounce. Bounce. "Sam said she was wearing a lilac dress that day."

Marly caught her breath. "He told you that?"

A little smile tilted the corner of Max's mouth. "He told me a lot of things, but for some reason, the color of her dress stood out in my mind."

"He must trust you a lot if he told you all that," Marly said.

He smiled again. "We have a lot in common. I'm sure that's why our friendship has developed so quickly."

"Like what?"

"Our profession for one thing. And our fathers, for another." He glanced up. "My father was a career army man, too. He was stationed at Fort Stanton when I was around fifteen. In fact, I remember hearing about your grandmother at the time it happened. Army bases are a lot like small towns. News travels fast." He paused. "You look a little pale, Marly. Why?"

"I didn't know you used to live here, that's all. I had no idea."

"After the old man was sent overseas, my mother and I moved back up north for a while. But I really liked it here. That's why I jumped at the opportunity to come back. In a strange way, I've always considered Mission Creek my home." When Marly didn't respond, he tilted his head. "You sure you're okay?"

Was he trying to tell her something? Marly wondered. Was he sending her some kind of message here? She summoned a smile. "Like I said, I'm just tired. Exhausted really. And I shouldn't take up any more of your time. Besides, I have to get back to the station." She turned toward the door, more than anxious to make good her escape. Suddenly being alone with Max Perry didn't seem like a good idea.

"Marly?"

Reluctantly, she glanced over her shoulder. "Yes?"

He bounced the pencil one last time on the desk, then caught it in his hand, as if to demonstrate how well he could manipulate his own reflexes. "You take care."

Their gazes locked for a moment, and Marly shuddered.

PATTY FUENTES HURRIED UP to Marly as she signed out at the station a little while later. "Did you hear?"

"Hear what?" Marly asked absently as she checked her name off the roster. "I just got here."

"There's been another suicide."

The pen fell from Marly's fingers as she glanced up. "Who? When?"

Patty shivered. "Crystal Bishop. A neighbor found her a little while ago and called it in. Navarro's on his way over there right now."

Marly didn't wait to hear the rest. She turned and

hit the door at a run. Darting across the parking lot, she climbed back into the squad car and headed across town, to the subdivision where Crystal Bishop lived.

All the way there, Patty's words kept echoing in Marly's head. Another suicide. Another suicide.

But Marly knew better. It wasn't suicide. It was murder.

She wondered for a moment if she should try to find Deacon. Their personal relationship aside, she needed his help. The whole town needed his help. The killer couldn't be stopped without him.

But something drew her to Crystal's house. Already dreading what she would see, Marly pulled to the curb behind Navarro's car and got out. Another squad car was in the driveway, and Marly knew there would be more arriving shortly. The whole Mission Creek Police Department would turn out for this.

A young deputy she barely knew was throwing up noisily in a flower bed as Marly crossed the yard. His partner, Pete Tenney, greeted Marly from the porch. "Another rough one, Jessop."

"Thanks for the warning," Marly murmured as she drew back the door and stepped inside

The house was dark and claustrophobic. Or maybe that was just her own frame of mind, Marly thought as she stopped for a moment to gather her nerve. "Chief Navarro?"

"Back here," he called out.

Marly followed his voice to the bathroom. The moment she glanced inside, she recoiled in horror.

The water had drained from the bathtub leaving Crystal Bishop slumped against the porcelain. Her eyes were open and her hands were lying, palms up, on her thighs so that Marly saw at once the deadly gashes across her wrists.

Most of the blood had gone down the drain with the water, but there was enough still to make Marly's stomach lurch.

Navarro knelt on the floor beside the tub. He glanced over his shoulder when he heard Marly gasp. "You ever see anything like this?"

Marly thought he was talking about Crystal's slashed wrists at first, but then her gaze lifted and she saw the writing on the mirror. It was on the walls and ceiling, too. She stared at it for a moment, unable to decipher the frantic scribbling. Then it came to her in a flash.

It was a message.

For her.

The same two desperate words were repeated over and over. *Gloomy Sunday…Gloomy Sunday… Gloomy Sunday…*

MARLY LEFT CRYSTAL BISHOP'S HOUSE and drove straight to Sam's. She wasn't even sure why. Maybe she just needed to see him, touch base with him, reaffirm her conviction that he couldn't have had anything to do with the deaths.

Or maybe it was because she could no longer deny that the words scrawled across Crystal Bishop's bathroom were a message for her.

*"…whether you want to admit it or not, you may be the only one who can stop it."*

Deacon's words came back to haunt her now as she pulled up in front of Sam's house. His Jeep wasn't in the driveway, but Marly supposed he could have parked in the garage. Deacon's truck was missing, too. She had no idea where he might be.

Marly sat for a moment, staring up at the white façade. This is where it had all started, she thought. With her grandmother's death. And maybe this was where Marly could find a way to end it.

She got out of the car and walked up to the porch. It had started to rain again, just as it had been raining that day fifteen years ago, and as Marly climbed the steps, she had the strangest sensation of déjà vu.

Her brother kept a spare key underneath a flowerpot on the front porch, but Marly didn't need to use it because the door was ajar. As she pulled back the screen and stepped inside her grandmother's house, it was like stepping back in time.

*"Grandma, you home? It's me, Marlene. I came over to see if you're okay. Mama was worried when you weren't in church this morning. Grandma?"*

Marly hesitated in the foyer. "Sam? You in here?"

The house was quiet. Unnaturally quiet. The same kind of silence Marly had noticed the day before in Gracie Abbott's home, and before that, at Ricky Morales's. A breathless, waiting stillness.

And then she heard the music.

Her blood froze as her gaze traveled up the stairs, and in that moment, Marly knew. She knew what she would find at the top. The killer was waiting for her in her grandmother's bedroom. Where it had all begun.

*"Grandma?"*

"Sam?"

There was still no answer, just the mournful wail of trumpets and the singer's achingly beautiful voice blending with the rain.

Slowly Marly climbed the stairs, glancing over her shoulder halfway up to make sure she wasn't leaving muddy footprints.

The door to her grandmother's bedroom was open, and as Marly stepped across the threshold, her gaze lifted. For a split second, she expected to see her grandmother…someone…hanging from the beam.

Instead her grandmother stood at the window.

Marly's heart beat so hard she could barely catch her breath. She couldn't possibly see…what she was seeing. Her grandmother was dead. Dead and buried and even a soul as hateful as Isabel Jessop's couldn't come back.

And yet…there she stood.

She had her back to the room, but Marly instantly recognized the lilac dress. Why wouldn't she? She'd seen that dress in her nightmares for years. And her grandmother's hair was just the way she remembered it, too. Drawn back and neatly done up in a French twist. As she turned her head slightly, Marly even saw the sparkle of those diamond earbobs…

Marly clutched the door frame as her knees threatened to buckle. But after that first moment of terror, she saw her mistake. The person at the window was taller, thinner, younger than her grandmother…

And then she turned.

"I knew you'd come."

That soft, familiar voice floated across the room and wrapped around Marly's throat like a noose. She had to struggle for breath. "Mama?" Her voice was little more than a gasping whisper.

"You found her, didn't you?"

"Who?" Marly managed.

"Crystal."

A fresh wave of fear rolled over Marly. "How did you—"

"I'm the one who called the police. I knew when you saw…you'd know. You'd figure it out. You'd find a way to stop it." She gave Marly a loving, tender smile. "My daughter, the cop."

"Mama, why?"

But her mother didn't answer. She was staring down at something she held in her hand. When she lifted it to the light, Marly saw that it was a gun. One of her father's pistols.

"Mama?"

She looked up in shock. "It's not for you, Marly. It was never meant for you. Or Sam. I would never hurt either one of you. But I wanted you to know." Her gaze rose to the ceiling beam where Marly had found her grandmother's body hanging fifteen years ago. "She was the first, you know."

Marly had to resist the urge to claw at her throat. She still felt as if she were suffocating. Drowning. "The first what?"

"The odd thing is, I never really meant for it to happen. I didn't even know...what I could do. It came as such a shock, Marly, you have no idea. That my own father could do that to me. Subject me to those terrible experiments. Turned me into someone...something...I didn't even recognize. They kept us in cages at that terrible place. We were nothing more than lab rats to them. They took away our free will. Destroyed our lives. We were just *children*."

Marly's heart was beating so hard she could hardly bear it. Her own mother had been subjected to the experiments Deacon had told her about. She tried to remember what else he'd told her.

*"I didn't find out about the children until much later, but from everything I've learned since, even the youngest were put through rigorous training and brainwashing techniques until they became adept at whatever special ability they showed an aptitude for. Then their memories were erased. The objective was to send them back home or back out into society until such time as they were needed."*

"Believe it or not, I was once a very strong person." Her mother smiled wistfully. "Willful, my father used to call me. Maybe that's why he did it."

Marly closed her eyes briefly. "Tell me about Grandma."

Andrea's smile disappeared. "She asked me to come over that morning before church. Demanded that I come over. When I got here, she was in rare form. Ranting and raving about the way I'd raised my children. You and Sam were a disgrace to the

Jessop name, she said. Then she accused you of stealing her diamond earrings. She was wearing them at the time, for God's sake. When I pointed that out to her, she just got meaner. She wouldn't shut up." Andrea paused to get her breath. "As I stood there listening to her, all I could think about was how much I hated her. How much I wanted her dead. I started fantasizing about how it would happen. She would take a belt from her closet, climb up on a chair, and hang herself in her own bedroom. The next thing I knew, she'd done exactly that."

Her gaze lifted again to the ceiling beam. "I was horrified by what I'd done. Terrified by what I knew I could do. The guilt became almost unbearable."

"Is that why you tried to kill yourself?"

She nodded. "But I couldn't go through with it. I couldn't leave you and Sam in Wesley's care. He was just like her."

"Is that why you stayed with him all these years?"

"That. And because he offered me protection. He knew what I'd been through. He promised he wouldn't let anything like that ever happen to me again."

"What about Joshua? What did he offer you."

Her mother's eyes glinted. "He offered me freedom. He made me happy. For the first time in my life, someone actually made me feel loved."

*But it's an illusion,* Marly wanted to cry. *A lie. Can't you see that?*

"The others…they wanted to take that away from me," her mother was saying. "I couldn't let that

happen. I couldn't go back…to the way it was before, trapped in that loveless marriage, living with
that cold, cruel man…''

A man very much like Joshua. That was the ultimate irony, Marly supposed. "What did you do?"

"What I'd been trained to do. Programmed to do.
In my desperation, it all came back to me. So easily
it was terrifying at first. But Gracie Abbott reminded
me so much of Isabel. Always berating me and
pointing out all my mistakes in front of Joshua. Always trying to make me look bad in his eyes. She
was a jealous, bitter old woman.''

"So you made her take her own life.''

"It was painless. She didn't suffer.''

*God,* Marly thought in horror. Were they really
having this conversation? Was this woman standing
before her truly her mother?

"What about Amber?''

"She had the one thing I could never have again.
Youth. Joshua told me that my age didn't matter,
but I knew if she kept throwing herself at him, it
would someday. How could it not? How could he
not start to compare us?''

"And David?''

"He was a mistake,'' her mother said with deep
regret. "He got in the way. He was at the wrong
place at the wrong time. He was my only mistake.''

Marly drew a shaky breath. "You killed Crystal
because she was having an affair with Joshua.''

"The affair was over, but she wouldn't leave him
alone. She wouldn't give us a chance.''

"That's what he told you?''

"And then Ricky Morales started making all those terrible threats against Joshua…"

"Oh, Mama."

"It's who I am, Marly. It's what they made me. But it has to end now. I wanted you to know so that you would understand." She lifted the gun. "I think you should leave now."

And suddenly Marly did understand. Everything. This was her mother's deathbed confession. "No," she whispered and started toward Andrea.

"Stay back," she warned. "I don't want to do this in front of you, but I will if I have to. It has to end, Marly. This is the only way."

The gun was at her mother's temple. Marly took another step toward her, but when Andrea's finger tightened on the trigger, she halted.

Marly didn't know what to do. She'd never felt so powerless in her life. She couldn't watch, and yet she didn't dare turn away. There had to be a way to stop her mother from doing this terrible thing. Even after everything Marly had found out today, she didn't want her mother to die. Not like this.

"Mama, please…"

Her mother's eyes widened in shock. She seemed to struggle for a moment with some terrible internal conflict, and then, almost in slow motion, her hand lowered to her side and the gun dropped to the floor. She bowed her head in defeat.

Only then was Marly aware that someone had come up behind her. She knew who it was before she turned.

# Chapter Sixteen

*One month later...*

The tiny courtyard at River Oaks Medical Center in San Antonio, Texas, was a quiet, restful spot and usually deserted in the late afternoons when Marly came to see her mother. Which was surprising, considering how lush and beautiful the place was, with its waterfalls and ferns and wild orchids. But then, Marly could understand why visitors might not want to linger too long at a psychiatric hospital, no matter how gorgeous the scenery.

For her, the courtyard was a good place to think. A good place to reflect on the past month and on her life in general. She'd come to terms with what her mother had done, and had even begun a fragile peace with her father. But there were other aspects of her life that still remained in turmoil. There were hidden parts of herself that Marly was only now daring to uncover.

Deacon had been right. She had erected a lot of

walls, and those walls did not come down easily, no matter how much she might wish for them to.

The wrought-iron gate creaked open, and Marly turned when someone called her name. "How did you know I was here?" she asked in surprise.

"One of the nurses saw you come out here." Sam sat down on the bench beside her. "Have you already been in to see her?"

Marly nodded. "It doesn't get any easier, does it?"

"No. But at least she's finally getting the help she's needed for a long, long time."

Marly drew a breath. "She's never going to leave this place, is she, Sam?"

"Probably not. She did some awful things, Marly. Ruined countless lives. It wouldn't be right for her to go free."

"I know." There was no way her mother could ever be prosecuted for what she'd done. A woman who could kill with her mind? No jury in the world would ever believe such a fantastic story.

The only alternative had been River Oaks. Deacon had suggested this particular hospital because one of the doctors on staff was an expert in dealing with the victims of Montauk.

Deacon had saved her mother's life that day, and then he'd just walked away. Marly hadn't heard from him since. And that was probably for the best. Or at least, she spent a lot of time trying to convince herself that it was.

"I ran into Navarro this morning," Sam was saying. "He told me you'd handed in your resignation. Why, Marly?"

She shrugged. "Because it's time to move on. Besides, I'm not cut out to be a cop, Sam. I'm not sure what I *am* cut out for. I haven't exactly found my niche, but maybe it's time I try a little harder to find it."

"Meaning?"

"There's a great big world out there. I think it's time I get out of Mission Creek and see some of it."

"You're not running away are you?"

"No. In fact, I think I've finally stopped running." She turned to stare up at him. "What about you?"

"I think I have found my niche," he said. "I love teaching. I have a home, some friends. It's not a perfect life, but it is a good one."

"And Dad? Are you ever going to be able to have a relationship with him?"

"Probably not. I know he didn't do those things to our mother, but he knew about them. He used her past to control her, to make her need him. And in case you've forgotten, he wasn't exactly a model father to us."

"I know that," Marly agreed. "But he is our father."

Sam merely shrugged.

After a moment, Marly took his hand. "I've always had a sense that you've been hiding something all these years. You knew about Mama, didn't you?"

"I suspected. I'd heard some things in the service. Rumors about secret experiments. Black ops teams that were associated with the Montauk Project back in Vietnam. I started doing some research. Putting a few things together. By the time I had it all figured out, though, it was too late to stop her."

"We were all too late." Marly squeezed his hand. "Can I ask you something?"

He turned to stare down at her. There was still something in his eyes, that stark loneliness that would always tear at Marly's heart.

"If you had another secret, something you wanted to talk about, you know you can come to me, don't you? You can tell me anything."

He smiled. "I'll keep that in mind. Right now, I'm not sure either one of us is ready for a heart-to-heart. We need some time to heal."

"I guess you're right."

He rose. "It's time for me to head back. You coming?"

"In a little while."

He turned to leave, then paused. "Promise you won't leave town without saying goodbye?"

"I promise."

"Good. I'm holding you to that."

After he left, Marly rested her head against the back of the bench and closed her eyes. She'd almost dozed off in the late afternoon sunshine when she heard the gate open again. Thinking it was Sam, she called out drowsily, "Forget something?"

"Yes, as a matter of fact."

At the sound of Deacon's voice, Marly's eyes

flew open and she spun. For a moment, she couldn't utter a word. Then she sputtered, "Wh-what are you doing here?"

"Looking for you." He crossed the narrow space between them and sat down beside her on the bench.

Marly's heart was beating so hard she could hardly breathe, let alone think. "Looking for me? Why?"

"Because I didn't like the way we left things, Marly. I think we've got a lot of unresolved issues between us."

"Such as?" she managed.

"Such as the fact that I haven't been able to eat or sleep since I left Mission Creek that day. I haven't been able to stop thinking about you for a single minute. You've got some kind of hold over me, and I want to know what it is."

The accusation took Marly completely by surprise. "I have a hold over you? You've got that backward, don't you? I'm not the one who can control thoughts and manipulate emotions. That night in my bedroom—"

"Didn't happen the way you think it did. I wasn't inside your head that night, Marly. I didn't manipulate anything, except…well." His smile sent a shiver straight up Marly's backbone.

"Then why did you let me think that you had?"

"Because I thought it was better that way. I thought you were right. I'd leave town and we'd forget all about each other. But it didn't work that way. At least not for me. There's something between us, Marly. Something…important."

Marly shivered again. She tried to tear her gaze from his, but couldn't.

"I care about you, Marly."

"I care about you, too," she admitted. "I've never felt this way about anyone before, but—"

"But?"

"I'm not sure I'm ready for it. Deacon, you scare me. This thing you can do with your mind..." She ran a hand through her short hair. "It's terrifying to think of someone having that kind of power over me."

"I understand that. I do. But what you don't seem to understand is that you're the one with all the power here. You're the one who has control over our future. You tell me to leave, I will. You tell me never to come back, I won't. But before you say anything I think you should know that..."

Marly caught her breath. "Yes?"

He took her hand. The contact made Marly's stomach flutter, made her heart beat even harder. "I'm already half in love with you. And falling harder every second I'm with you."

Marly was stunned by the confession. Blindsided by all the emotions storming through her. She didn't know how to respond, what to say. She lifted her gaze to his. "I'm the one in control? *I* have power over *you?*"

"You have no idea."

She swallowed. "And...you say you're willing to abide by whatever I decide?"

"You have my word."

"In that case, kiss me," she said. "And don't stop until I say so."

"Already the power is going to your head," he murmured. But he moved in closer without hesitation until his lips were only inches from hers.

Marly put a hand on his chest to hold him back. "There's something I should probably tell you first. I think I'm falling in love with you, too."

And then it was a very long time before either of them spoke again.

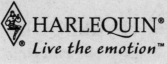

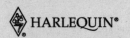

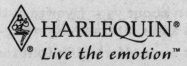

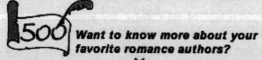

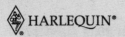

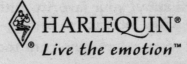

**Coming in March 2004
to Silhouette Books**

Widower Harrison Parker needed a nanny for
his three young children so he could work on a
top-secret government project. But he hadn't
counted on finding such a beautiful and intriguing
woman, who just might capture his heart....

Five extraordinary siblings.
One dangerous past.
Unlimited potential.

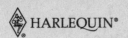

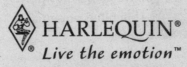